The Christmas Cards

An Amish Holiday Romance

Sylvia Price

Penn and Ink Writing, LLC

Contents

Stay Up-to-Date with Sylvia Price

Subscribe to Sylvia's newsletter at newsletter.sylviaprice.com to get to know Sylvia and her family. It's also a great way to stay in the loop about new releases, freebies, promos, and more.

As a thank-you, you will receive several FREE exclusive short stories that aren't available for purchase.

Praise for Sylvia Price's Books

"Author Sylvia Price wrote a storyline that enthralled me. The characters are unique in their own way, which made it more interesting. I highly recommend reading this book. I'll be reading more of Author Sylvia Price's books."

"You can see the love of the main characters and the love that the author has for the main characters and her writing. This book is so wonderful. I cannot wait to read more from this beautiful writer."

"The storyline caught my attention from the very beginning and kept me interested throughout the entire book. I loved the chemistry between the characters."

"A wonderful, sweet and clean story with strong characters. Now I just need to know what happens next!"

"First time reading this author, and I'm very impressed! I love feeling the godliness of this story."

"This was a wonderful story that reminded me of a glorious God we have."

"I encourage all to read this uplifting story of faith and friendship."

"I love Sylvia's books because they are filled with love and faith."

Other Books by Sylvia Price

Elijah: An Amish Story of Crime and Romance
– http://getbook.at/elijah

Seeds of Spring Love (Amish Love Through the Seasons Book 1) –
http://getbook.at/seedsofspring

Sprouts of Summer Love (Amish Love Through the Seasons Book 2)
– http://getbook.at/sproutsofsummer

Fruits of Fall Love (Amish Love Through the Seasons Book 3) – http://getbook.at/fruitsoffall

Waiting for Winter Love (Amish Love Through the Seasons Book 4) – http://getbook.at/waitingforwinter

Amish Love Through the Seasons Boxed Set (The Complete Series) –
http://getbook.at/amishseasons

The Christmas Arrival – http://getbook.at/christmasarrival

Jonah's Redemption: Book 1 – FREE
Jonah's Redemption: Book 2 – http://getbook.at/jonah2
Jonah's Redemption: Book 3 – http://getbook.at/jonah3
Jonah's Redemption: Book 4 – http://getbook.at/jonah4
Jonah's Redemption: Book 5 – http://getbook.at/jonah5

Jonah's Redemption: Boxed Set – http://getbook.at/jonahset

Songbird Cottage Beginnings (Pleasant Bay Prequel) – FREE
The Songbird Cottage (Pleasant Bay Book 1) –
http://getbook.at/songbirdcottage
Return to Songbird Cottage (Pleasant Bay Book 2) –
http://getbook.at/returntosongbird
Escape to Songbird Cottage (Pleasant Bay Book 3) –
http://getbook.at/escapetosongbird
Secrets of Songbird Cottage (Pleasant Bay Book 4) –
http://getbook.at/secretsofsongbird
Seasons at Songbird Cottage (Pleasant Bay Book 5) –
http://getbook.at/seasonsatsongbird
*The Songbird Cottage Boxed Set (Pleasant Bay Complete
Series Collection)* – http://getbook.at/songbirdbox

*The Crystal Crescent Inn (Sambro Lighthouse
Book 1)* – http://getbook.at/cci1
*The Crystal Crescent Inn (Sambro Lighthouse
Book 2)* – http://getbook.at/cci2
*The Crystal Crescent Inn (Sambro Lighthouse
Book 3)* – http://getbook.at/cci3
*The Crystal Crescent Inn (Sambro Lighthouse
Book 4)* – http://getbook.at/cci4
*The Crystal Crescent Inn (Sambro Lighthouse
Book 5)* – http://getbook.at/cci5
*The Crystal Crescent Inn Boxed Set (Sambro Lighthouse
Complete Series Collection)* – http://getbook.at/ccibox

Part One

Chapter One: Everything You Do and Everything You Are

It was much too early for anyone to be traveling on the old road into town. Even the farmers, who rose with the sun, would only now be pulling on their boots and steadily tying their laces. Yet someone was walking along that old road and could spy the figure of a young woman standing at her bedroom window. She wore a white nightgown and a heavy knit shawl about her shoulders. As she stared out into the dawn light, the young woman pulled her shawl tightly around her body. It looked to the traveler as if she were trying to hold herself together.

Lucy Yoder could feel the iciness of the outside air pressing against the glass beneath her hand. It twitched. She wanted to open the window so that she might feel something—coldness, perhaps, or frostbite against her skin—anything but the incessant numbness that had robbed her of her senses. Instead, Lucy turned away from the window and exhaled. The bedroom before her was dressed in muted shades of cream, but her eyes moved to the small, illustrated calendar hanging on the western wall. For thirty days, Lucy had awoken to the very same picture. It was of an old barn surrounded by bare trees—an unremarkable illustration, save for the group of children who sat in a pile of leaves beneath the naked oaks and maples. All wore woolen hats and mittens, faces flushed, and smiles, frozen. But in the filtered morning light, Lucy slowly peeled the month of November away.

That morning marked the first day of December, and the picture of the old barn, bare trees, and laughing children was replaced by a picture of a snowy landscape, pines frosted with snow, and birches dressed in layers of twinkling ice. The children were gone, leaving without a trace, a lifeless snowman betraying their presence.

∞∞∞∞

Lucy's mind drifted back to a day in late May. She closed her eyes, sighing wistfully. The weather had been perfect on the day, not too warm. A delicate breeze had tickled the new leaves to make them dance playfully on their stems. Albrecht had held her hand as they'd ambled lazily along the lake's shoreline. The water had sparkled beneath the glorious sun's bright rays. Though months had passed, Lucy could still feel the warmth of sun on her face and the affection of her husband. She could still hear the children laughing nearby, their shoes and socks cast away so they might dip their toes in the cool water.

The couple had walked beneath an old weeping willow. As they did, Lucy had looked up to see a little brown bird perched on the branch above them.

"Tell me what you are thinking," Albrecht had gently pressed.

"Why do you want to know?" Lucy had rejoined.

Albrecht had smiled because he knew what he would say next. It was the same answer he gave her every time she asked him that question. "Because I wish to know everything that you do and to understand everything that you are."

Lucy had smiled. "I was just thinking how rare this kind of happiness is and how, sometimes, being this happy scares me. Does that sound silly?"

Albrecht had shaken his head. "*Nee*, I don't think it sounds silly. Nothing lasts forever, so it's important to feel everything as it comes to you, good and bad."

Lucy had looked up at Albrecht, and as she'd stared into his green eyes, she'd wondered how it was possible to love someone so much. "Are you happy?"

"How can you possibly ask me that? You know how much I love you."

"And are you scared?"

"Sometimes," Albrecht had admitted. "But not right now. Right now, all I want to do is hold my *fraa's* hand and walk with her under the spring sun."

Lucy had agreed by squeezing Albrecht's hand. He was so much better than she was at living in the moment.

"*Gut*," Albrecht had said as he kissed the top of her head.

The young couple had continued on their walk, and as they had approached the head of the lake, Albrecht had stopped and smiled. "You should see this lake in wintertime. You see how only the ripples shimmer in the sun? Well, in the wintertime, the whole lake is like a mirror that perfectly reflects the sky above it, and the air is so quiet that you can hear your own heart-beat if you listen close enough." Albrecht's eyes had shone as he spoke. His passion was infectious.

Lucy had looked out across the scene before them. She reveled in the dancing leaves, the water lapping at the shoreline, and the flapping of birds' wings, which were imprinted in her memory. It had seemed impossible to imagine the stillness that winter would someday bring.

"I can't imagine it," Lucy had admitted. "It's just all so very much alive at this moment."

"We will come in December," Albrecht had promised. "Then you will see what I mean. The world freezes beneath your very feet, and it's as if time itself stands still."

Lucy had imagined them on the lake together, arm in arm, twirling across the ice as their shadows danced beneath them.

∞ ∞ ∞

A clattering in the kitchen returned the young widow to the present—now December—where the harsh reality was that she and Albrecht would never skate arm-in-arm on the icy lake. Alone in a cold bedroom, Lucy quickly turned away from the calendar and hurried to the wardrobe where she had laid out her clothes the night prior. Ever since she was a young girl, Lucy had always hated dressing in the wintertime and had learned to dress quickly. She emerged from her bedroom and sauntered toward the racket coming from the kitchen in record time.

"*Gude mariye,*" Lucy said quietly, standing in the kitchen doorway.

Eleanor Yoder turned around and gave her a warm smile. "*Gude mariye,* Lucy. How did you sleep?"

"Well," replied Lucy.

Eleanor did not believe her daughter-in-law though she did not let on. Lucy had purple shadows beneath her eyes, which seemed to have darkened overnight. Her face was pale. Also, Eleanor had heard her crying in the night, but she knew better than to push her daughter-in-law, so she chose to say nothing.

"Would you like me to get started on the bread?" Lucy asked.

"*Danki*," Eleanor agreed.

Lucy gave her mother-in-law a strained smile and walked across the kitchen to the wooden table. Eleanor had already laid out what they needed. Lucy picked up the pot of wheat flour and sprinkled a light coat across the table. As always, the bread dough had been prepared the night before and left to stand. It now sat in a bowl covered by a white cloth. When Lucy had finished dusting the table with flour, she removed the cloth and scraped the dough onto the floured surface. As she kneaded, she thought of nothing other than the bread. Blessed routines allowed her to forget about everything else.

As Lucy kneaded, Eleanor kept an eye on her. She twice caught the young woman pulling her gray shawl around her body. It was as though she were afraid of falling to pieces on the kitchen floor.

Chapter Two: The Trip into Town

"I can go into town," Lucy volunteered.

They had all just finished breakfast and were seated at the sunny table that stood against the eastern wall of the kitchen. Eleanor and her husband, Moses Yoder, were discussing which supplies they needed from town. Lucy's mind had been elsewhere. Nevertheless, she had caught the end of the conversation in which they were trying to decide who would go.

"Are you sure you are up for it?" Eleanor asked.

Lucy nodded. Eleanor's eyes were on her as if to say, *You're too tired.* Lucy did not wish to spend the morning being scrutinized and assessed. She wanted to get out of the house, and going into town seemed like the perfect excuse to escape for a while. "It would be nice to get some fresh air."

"Let the girl go," Moses interjected. "She hasn't been out of the house in days."

Lucy felt her face grow warm. Her father-in-law was right. She had not been anywhere in quite some time.

"Well, that would be very helpful," Eleanor conceded. "Moses is busy on the farm most of the day, and I have a hundred things to get on with here."

Eleanor rose from the table and began carrying the breakfast dishes to the sink. Lucy stood up to help, but Eleanor stopped her. "Don't worry about those now, *Liewi*. I will get to them later. You go and get ready, and I'll draw up a list for you."

Lucy nodded and excused herself from the table. She headed back to her room to fetch her winter coat, gloves, and *kapp*. As she left her room, she caught sight of the calendar. Her stomach sank. She quickly closed her bedroom door behind her and went back downstairs.

"Here," Eleanor said, handing her the list. "Moses was all for sending you to the farm supply store to get what he needed, but I told him that it would probably be best if he made a separate trip."

Lucy smiled gratefully. She had not grown up in a farming family, and while she had learned a lot since moving to the Yoder farm, she still did not feel confident buying any sort of farm supplies. She also knew that Moses was particular. Lucy had enough on her plate without picking a fight with Moses.

"Are you sure you feel well enough to go into town?" Eleanor asked again. "It's a fair walk."

Lucy nodded. She was used to Eleanor's mothering. Thus, she made haste before the lady changed her mind and decided to go herself—or to accompany the girl. "I will see you later."

Lucy hurried to the front door with the shopping list clutched tightly in her hand. She opened the front door and stepped out. A southerly wind hit her. She teared up, making her look the mourning widow she was. She quickly descended the porch steps before the cold drove her back inside and headed down the narrow path toward the farm gate.

The road from the Yoders' farm into town was over a mile long, but Lucy was in no rush. Her dangling basket connected with her hip, but she didn't care. The frozen world around her beckoned. It had been late autumn since Lucy had taken this path. The leaves then had been vibrant reds, yellows, and oranges on the trees. Now the trees stood nude, their brown leaves littered about their trunks. The softness of autumn had ceded way to the hardness of winter. The morning light was still golden though it did nothing to temper the icy landscape.

As she walked, Lucy pulled her coat tightly around her body. She looked to the east and spotted a large, wooden barn. Lucy felt her breath catch in her chest as her mind unwittingly went back to the day that she had first stepped into that barn. That was the day that she had met Albrecht Yoder.

Before she was Lucy Yoder, she had been Lucy Bontrager, a shopkeeper's daughter for a small community in east Indiana. She was the only child of Jeremiah and Naomi Bontrager and had grown up in a good home. Her parents, although firm disciplinarians, had raised their daughter to be true to the ordinances of *Gott.* What a blessing it was, therefore, to have a child who gladly obeyed. Lucy's life followed a smooth path, with nothing remarkable ever to have happened. She had hoped that one day, it might.

Like many girls her age, Lucy had dreamed of meeting the man with whom *Gott* would wish her to marry and start a family. Yet, no matter how much she had longed for such a future, it had not materialized. She knew that all things would happen in *Gott's* time if she was obedient to His will, so she'd busied herself with her daily chores, the routine occupying her as she waited.

For months, Lucy had watched as the girls her age had coupled off and planned their weddings. She was left alone. As she lay in bed at night, Lucy would stare up at the ceiling and wonder if there was someone out there for her or if her destiny did not include marriage and a family of her own.

Just after Lucy's seventeenth birthday, her best friend, Hannah, arrived on her porch.

"Please, Lucy, you have to come," Hannah had insisted. "All of the boys from the neighboring communities will be there."

Lucy was pensive, a guise she used to hide apprehension. She'd never been to a *sing* before, an occasion when the youths from several neighboring districts would come together for a Sunday afternoon to sing hymns. It was usually hosted in a family barn and was an opportunity for young men and women to meet one another in a chaperoned environment that was acceptable to *Gott*.

"When is it?" Lucy had asked.

"Sunday at four o'clock."

Hannah, like Lucy, had also had no luck in finding love, but unlike Lucy, Hannah was outgoing.

"As long as my *daed* and *maem* agree," Lucy had offered.

Hannah had squealed and thrown her arms around Lucy.

That Sunday, Mr. Bontrager had escorted Lucy and Hannah to their neighboring community in his buggy. When they'd arrived at the barn, Mr. Bontrager had remained in his seat as the girls climbed down. He was to wait for the *sing* to be over and then drive them home.

Lucy had looked around and seen that there were various other buggies parked around the barn too.

"Come on," Hannah had said, excitedly. She'd grabbed Lucy's hand and dragged her across the grass and into the large barn. Upon entering the stable, they had spotted a long table in the middle of the space. There were no chairs, just a long table.

"That's where we stand," Hannah had said as she pointed to one side of the table. "And the boys stand on the other side."

Lucy had nodded. Nerves had kept her mute. The knots in her stomach had threatened to keep her off her feet. More people had poured in.

"Don't look so worried, Lucy," Hannah had teased. "You have a lovely singing voice."

Lucy had grimaced.

"Come on," Hannah had said. "Let's find a place." Hannah had led the way with Lucy following, and people had taken positions around the table. Lucy and Hannah had found spots near the middle, and they'd stood in silence until the table was full.

"*Willkumm* everyone," someone had announced. A tall, young man had stood at the head of the table. "My name is Daniel. If everyone has found a place, then we can begin."

"That's Daniel Fisher," a girl had whispered to her friend. "This is his family's barn."

"For those of you who have never been to a *sing*, let me explain how it works," Daniel had continued. "Anyone who wants to suggest a hymn to sing may do so by raising a hand. The first hand up gets to go first. Once the song had been chosen, we start to sing. Quite simple, *ya*?"

General murmurs of agreement from both sides of the table had sounded.

"This is going to be so much fun," Hannah had whispered as she squeezed Lucy's hand.

"Now, before we start singing, I think that we should each first introduce ourselves to the person across from us," Daniel had instructed.

Lucy, who had not taken her eyes off of Daniel, had then looked at the boy standing before her. He'd been the prettiest boy she had ever seen. Long, dark eyelashes had framed his green eyes. His black hair had looked neatly disheveled as if it had fallen every which way in its intended place. Lucy had felt her cheeks burn under his gaze.

"*Gude daag*," he had said warmly. "My name is Albrecht Yoder."

"*Gude daag*," Lucy had said shyly. So captivated was she that she'd been unable to think.

"Tell him your name," Hannah had hissed.

"Lucy," she had mumbled. "Lucy Bontrager."

"*Ich bin froh dich zu aadreffe* (Pleased to meet you), Lucy Bontrager." His smile had reached the corners of his eyes.

Lucy had wished that she were as composed and confident as Hannah, not a red-faced, mumbling mess. She'd been relieved when Daniel had suddenly spoken again and had looked away only to regain her composure.

"Okay, now that we are all on a first-name basis, let the *sing* begin."

A few hands had shot straight up in the air. Daniel had chosen a tall girl near the end of the table. She'd chosen a hymn that Lucy knew well. A moment later, the room had broken out into song.

Albrecht had gazed at Lucy. His stare had made her shy, so she had not sung the first verse. The chorus, however, lifted her soul, so she had sung like a sparrow.

The evening had passed by quickly. Lucy had looked around the room and noticed that everyone was filled with the light and joy of the Lord. The last hymn, "God be With You Till We Meet Again," was one of Lucy's favorites. As she'd sung, she looked across the table at Albrecht to catch his eye.

When she had, the entire room had disappeared, leaving just them, singing to one another. Lucy had known, then and there, that she wanted to marry that boy. As the chorus of voices had reached a decrescendo, the last note had hung in the air.

Albrecht had leaned across the table and asked in a low voice, "Will you come again?"

"I don't know," Lucy had confessed.

"I hope you will."

Lucy had tried to tell him how much she had enjoyed meeting him and how she, too, hoped to see him again, but her words had been drowned by the sea of chatter that marked the end of the *sing*. The youths had then made their way toward the doors.

"Come on, Luce," Hannah had said.

Lucy had given Albrecht one last smile before following her friend out of the barn.

The next *sing* was a fortnight thence. Lucy had sat beside her father on the buggy and had thought of nothing but seeing Albrecht again. The two weeks had dragged. It had taken so long that Lucy was convinced the sun had slowed its pace across the sky. Lucy's mind had jumped from one anxious thought to the next. She had feared that the *sing* would be canceled or that Albrecht had met a girl he liked better. All of these possibilities had plagued Lucy, and so by the time they'd been scheduled to attend the next *sing*, Lucy had made herself sick with worry.

"Don't worry," Hannah had whispered as they sat side-by-

THE CHRISTMAS CARDS (THE COMPLETE SERIES)

side in her father's buggy. "He will be there."

"What if everything was in my head?" Lucy had groaned.

"I saw the way that he was looking at you. There is no way that it was all in your head."

Lucy had squeezed her best friend's hand in gratitude.

Upon arrival at the *sing*, Lucy had craned her neck, trying to spot Albrecht at the table. He was absent.

"He'll be here," Hannah had reassured her. "We are earlier than most people, today."

Lucy had kept her eyes glued to the door. There had still been no sign of Albrecht. Convinced that it had been all for naught, Lucy had bowed her head to blink back her tears. Gravity, however, had thwarted her efforts.

A stranger had stood across the table from the Bontrager girl as they took their places, his shadow looming large though his smile had been warm. Lucy had been unable to find it in her heart to return his smile.

"He's not coming," Lucy had mumbled.

"He might just be late," Hannah had replied.

"*Gude daag*," Daniel had greeted warmly. "*Willkumm!*"

Lucy had listened to him explain the rules of the *sing*. When he'd instructed everyone to greet the person opposite him or her, Lucy had not looked up.

"*Gude daag*," a voice had whispered from across the table. "I'm Albrecht Yoder."

Lucy had looked up, incredulous. The stranger had gone. A smiling Albrecht had taken his place.

"I thought you weren't coming," Lucy had stammered, her tears transformed to joy.

"I wouldn't miss an opportunity to see you again," Albrecht

had reassured her.

Lucy had beamed. She had sung like a canary welcoming in the morning, her shyness having vanished in the light of Albrecht's smile. With her eyes locked onto his countenance, her spirits had soared. She had sung to her God as though He were standing before her.

During the break, merry chatter had ensued. Hannah had talked animatedly with the boy across from her. Lucy had been happy for her friend, who, like her, had been desperate to find love.

"Tell me something," Albrecht had asked.

"What?" Lucy had encouraged him, batting her eyes and grinning.

"Anything. I just want to hear the sound of your voice. What do your parents do?"

"They own a shop in town. And yours?"

"We have a farm not far from here."

Lucy had nodded. She was unsurprised. Albrecht looked like a farmer's son: tanned hands and face, broad shoulders that could have carried a donkey around them, and biceps the size of a stovepipe.

"Do you have a beau?" Albrecht had asked.

Lucy had flushed. *Nee,* she had mouthed, shaking her head for added emphasis.

"I was hoping you would say that."

Daniel had called for silence just as Lucy's heart had skipped a beat. The *sing* had resumed then.

That evening had ended much too soon. Before Lucy could go, Albrecht had asked her to stay.

"I'll wait by the doors," Hannah had said. She'd winked before attending her post.

Lucy had given her a grateful smile and then turned to Albrecht. The farm boy had looked just as nervous as she, breathing slowly before he spoke.

"I've been looking forward to seeing you for two weeks. I was wondering if, after the next *sing*, I might give you a ride home in my buggy."

Every Amish girl knew what a ride home in a boy's buggy meant—they would then officially be a couple. Lucy had only dreamed of experiencing that rite of passage, which she thought had, sadly, passed her by. Lucy had not answered immediately.

"What do you think?"

"I will have to ask my parents," Lucy had finally managed. "If they agree, then I would very much like to ride in your buggy *to* the next *sing*." The girl had not been able to believe her boldness! Hannah must have rubbed off on her.

Albrecht's face had cracked into an infectious grin, which Lucy had only been able to mirror. She had never imagined that she would find being with someone so easy. With Albrecht, nothing had seemed hard or complicated. It was like breathing; she didn't need to think about it, it just happened.

"I'll write to you," Albrecht had promised. "Until we meet again." He had tipped his hat, turned on his heel, and strolled off.

∞∞∞

Approaching horse hooves returned the young widow back to her present stroll into town. She scurried off to the side, allowing the buggy to pass. A young man tipped his hat to her. Lucy obliged him with an anemic smile.

Lucy arrived in town shortly after eight o'clock in the morning, but it was already bustling like rush hour since the community did not waste the day. Having her head down and her unwillingness to make eye contact only fueled the gossip. The elderly were terrible whisperers. Lucy wished that she had not volunteered to come into town that morning. It was not in their custom to mourn in public. It was customary to smile and return greetings when in town. Thus, clothed in grief, strolling through the center of town with her head drooped, made her stand out in the same way she would at a rock concert. She was exhausted by the time she reached the general store. As she opened the door, a little silver bell tinkled merrily, alerting everyone in the packed store to her presence.

"*Gude mariye,*" a voice called.

Lucy turned around to see the storeowner's wife smiling at her. Lucy returned her smile, but she did not speak, as she could not remember her name.

"Let me know if you need any help," the woman offered.

"*Danki,*" Lucy mumbled. She unfolded the list and made her way about the store. Unfamiliar with the layout, the girl who wished to be invisible meandered about the shop like a bunny grazing, sometimes looking down, most often looking up to see if anyone was watching, hopping about the market to the next patch of clover. It was on one such occasion, while searching for a jar of molasses, that she overheard two women whispering in the next aisle.

"What is she still doing here? Why has she not returned home to her family?"

"I don't know. It is strange. You'd think she'd want to go

home after something like that."

"Well, we all thought that she was rather strange when Albrecht brought her home."

Lucy had not realized that she was holding her breath until the footsteps behind her made her gasp. Desperate to leave, the young widow quickly gathered the last of the items and made her way to the counter.

"Did you find everything you needed?" the storeowner's wife asked.

"*Ya, danki,*" Lucy replied.

The older woman unpacked everything from the basket and methodically wrote each of the items down in a ledger. Once she was done, she repacked everything. "There you go."

"*Danki,*" Lucy said, taking the basket from the woman. Payment was, as yet, unnecessary, for the Yoders ran an account that was paid at the end of the month.

"Please send Mrs. Yoder my best wishes."

"I will," Lucy agreed, then headed out. As she did, she caught the eyes of the two women who had been whispering about her, and they both offered her sympathetic smiles that Lucy chose to ignore. She walked quickly until she was on the outskirts of town. There, she slowed, contemplated the nature about her, and let her ears listen once more. The singing sparrows cheered her heart. *It's much better than hearing two old ladies chatter on and on about me,* she thought. The basket was heavy, so she alternated in switching it from her right arm to her left arm, sometimes setting it down. Lucy wished not to think about what she had overheard, but the conversation would not leave her mind. The women were probably just curious and had meant no harm. But who likes to be thought of as strange?

Lucy was still new to the settlement. She and Albrecht had not yet settled in his hometown before he died. She struggled to fit in, shyness being her handicap. The Amish are a social bunch, so a newcomer who does not make small talk and who keeps her head down made Lucy something of a pariah. Though Albrecht had passed, she was determined to make a life for herself where they had planned to settle, out of sheer stubbornness rather than reason.

Shortly after Albrecht's death, Lucy's parents had asked her to return home, but she'd refused.

"Why?" her mother had asked. "Come home and heal."

"I can't," Lucy had confessed.

When her parents had asked her for a reason, Lucy told them that she had her reasons.

Bitterly disappointed, her parents left to recruit the help of Lucy's childhood friend. A week later, she'd received a letter from Hannah.

Dear Lucy,

Your parents tell me that you don't wish to come home. I cannot begin to understand what you are going through, but I wish you would reconsider coming home. We miss you.

Your friend always,
Hannah

The letter had broken Lucy's heart. She did not want her family and friends to think that she did not wish to return home, so her reply had been swift.

Dear Hannah,

Danki *for your letter. I do not wish you, nor my parents, to think that my reluctance to return home has anything to do with you. There are several reasons why I cannot come.*

First, when Albrecht was just eight years old, his older brothers were crushed when a tractor overturned on the farm. Albrecht was the only one left, and now, he's gone too. This new pain opened old wounds for my in-laws. I must stay with them. I cannot ask them to suffer another loss so soon.

Furthermore, I am not ready to leave. I can still feel Albrecht here, Hannah—in the house where he grew up, in the garden he used to work, near the lake where we used to walk. When I walk into our bedroom, I see the pencil marks where Albrecht and his brothers recorded their heights as youngsters. I can imagine Albrecht standing impatiently while his brothers measured his height and laughed at him for being short. When I open the closet in our room, I can still smell Albrecht. You know that old, straw hat, the one that I threatened to throw out all those times? It's still hanging on its hook by the door. I am not ready to leave even the smallest part of Albrecht behind. That is why I can't come home. Each day brings countless memories to relive and new discoveries about the husband with whom I'll never grow old.

Share my reasons with my parents if you think it will help them. I have not since I am unsure that they will understand. Their joy blinds them to my sorrow.

I miss you, Hannah.

Your friend always,
Lucy

Chapter Three: The Christmas Card

ucy climbed the porch steps, drained both physically and emotionally. The gossip from the old ladies weighed down her every step, and the basket was over-filled. She wished to crawl under the covers and go to sleep.

As Lucy reached the front door, she noticed a cream envelope on the mat at her feet. She knelt to retrieve it. Her name was written on it. She turned the envelope around in her hands, looking for an address or some other indication as to who might have sent it, but there was nothing. Lucy had placed her basket on the ground to open it when she heard Eleanor calling from inside.

"Lucy? Is that you?"

Lucy stashed the envelope into her coat pocket. She let herself in and marched down the hallway to the kitchen. There stood her mother-in-law. Eleanor's apron and arms were covered in flour as she kneaded the dough for their lunchtime loaf. She looked up as Lucy stepped into the room and smiled at her.

"How did it go?"

"Fine," Lucy said as she set the basket down and began to unpack it.

"Did you see Mrs. Stoltzfus?"

That was her name! Lucy thought, picturing the storeowner's wife in her mind. "*Ya.* She asked me to send you her best wishes."

Eleanor smiled and continued to knead the dough as if trying to extract a confession. Lucy finished unpacking, unwilling to say more.

"Why don't you go and lie down before lunch?" Eleanor suggested when Lucy was finished.

"Don't you need my help to prepare lunch?" Lucy asked.

Eleanor shook her head. "I am almost finished here, and I was just going to use the leftover meatloaf from last night, so it's hardly any trouble. Go lie down for a bit, and I will call you when lunch is ready."

Lucy retreated from the kitchen and headed to her room. She was grateful to have a moment to rest and for Eleanor's thoughtfulness. She lay on her back and stared up at the ceiling. Just on the cusp of sleep, the memory of the mysterious envelope jolted her awake.

Lucy swung her legs over the edge of the bed and walked across the room to where her coat hung on the back of the chair. She reached into the pocket and retrieved the envelope. Lucy returned to the bed and sat on the edge. She paused, turning the envelope over in her hands once more, smelling it, and gazing at it. Finally, she pulled the card from its envelope. The front of the card revealed a winter's scene. The tiny details were so precise and perfect that for a moment, Lucy thought it was a photograph, but upon closer inspection, she realized that the Christmas card had been painted. Christmas cards were popular among their communities, and she had sent and received many during her life, but none had been as beautiful as this one. The painted scene depicted a frozen lake, which reflected the blue sky above it as if it were a mirror. On the lake were skaters, who wore bright smiles and whose cheeks were pink from the cold. The trees and grounds surrounding the lake were dusted in a layer of powdery snow.

Lucy lifted her finger and delicately traced the details of the people's faces to see if they felt as real as they looked. The scene was precisely what she had imagined when Albrecht had promised to take her skating. It was what their lake would look like in the winter. It had the same stillness and fragile beauty her late husband had described. Lucy, hesitant to look away from the skating scene but curious to know who had sent her such a beautiful card, opened it.

No winter lasts forever
No spring skips its turn.
Your grief will pale as the seasons pass,
You will know happiness again soon.

There was no name or signature, only the initial "A." Lucy stared at the letter, unable to fathom who would send a card without leaving a name.

Eleanor's light rap on the door interrupted Lucy's ponderings. "Lunch is ready."

"Coming," Lucy replied. She folded the card to stuff it the drawer of her nightstand. She then headed to the kitchen.

"How was your trip into town?" Moses asked as they ate their meatloaf sandwiches.

"Fine," Lucy said, echoing her earlier response.

"*Gut,*" Moses said.

The room fell silent, and Lucy's mind was still on the mysterious Christmas card. She was not entirely oblivious to the fact that Eleanor and Moses did not seem to be talking to one another. Lucy noticed but brushed it off since everything had seemed fine at breakfast.

A few minutes later, Moses pushed back his chair loudly and stood up. He clearly wanted his exit to be noticed. *"Danki* for the sandwich," he said stiffly before leaving the room through the back door.

Lucy watched him go, then turned to Eleanor who was busy stacking the plates. "Eleanor!"

Ignoring Lucy, Eleanor carried the dishes to the sink. Lucy got up and walked over to her. She watched her mother-in-law scrub the plates, hands trembling.

"Let me do that," Lucy offered.

"*Nee*, I'm fine," Eleanor insisted, her voice cracking.

"Did something happen?"

Eleanor sighed. "Moses and I had an argument. I think he is working too hard and should hire some new farmhands, but he will hear nothing of the sort." This was unsurprising. Moses had been working his fingers to the bone to keep on top of the farm work ever since Albrecht died. Eleanor had asked him several times to consider hiring help, but he had always refused.

"It wasn't supposed to be like this," Eleanor said. "They were supposed to be here to help their *daed*." She scrubbed a bowl harder for emphasis. It was all that she could do to hold it together. After all, the Yoder line was over now. "He doesn't want anyone but his *seh* (sons)," Eleanor continued. "It'll kill him, all this work, and I can't bear to lose anyone else." Eleanor wept, her tears rolling down her long face, salty drops lost in the sink of soapy water.

Lucy put her arms around her mother-in-law's shoulders and held her tightly. The woman would not turn to cry on Lucy's shoulder. Her husband had rubbed off on her—too strong to be pitied, but too weak to seek help.

"I'm sorry," Eleanor said. "You don't need to hear an old woman's woes. Not when you have your own grief."

"You can always talk to me," Lucy said.

Eleanor smiled weepily, her face cracking, seeping sorrow. She wiped it away with the bottom of her apron. Both women sniffled.

"Can I do anything to help?" Lucy asked.

"*Nee*," Eleanor said. "You have done more than enough. Moses and I will work things out. We always do."

Lucy nodded. The pain of losing one man was hard enough. To triple it and risk losing more was a depth of sorrow unfathomable to the young widow. Without knowing what else to do, she fetched a red-and-white-checkered tea towel and dried the dishes. Neither spoke as they worked.

Once finished, they both retired to the sitting room. Lucy lit the fire in the grate and then joined Eleanor in sewing. Despite her best efforts, Lucy could not concentrate on her needlework. Her thoughts danced between Eleanor's woes and the beautiful Christmas card, which now sat in her bedside drawer.

Chapter Four: Pieces of You

By the time dinner arrived, the argument between Eleanor and Moses had blown over. Eleanor smiled at him as she placed his plate down in front of him. He thanked her warmly. Lucy was relieved that Eleanor's sadness and Moses' anger had abated for the time being.

Lucy offered to do the washing up after dinner so that Eleanor and Moses could retreat to the sitting room. As she washed the dishes, it felt as though Albrecht were standing next to her. She basked in it. Once finished, she beckoned her late husband's presence to follow her to prepare the dough for the morning loaf. Such sorrowful comfort. *Did the painting look like what you wanted to show me?* she asked. Lucy listened for an answer. She finished with the dough and covered it with a clean cloth, setting it beside the warm coal stove. She washed her hands and headed to the sitting room.

As Lucy approached the sitting room, she could hear Eleanor and Moses speaking softly to one another. *Perhaps they could use the time alone?* Lucy wondered. She decided to break with tradition (of joining them after dinner) and ask to be excused.

"Are you quite all right?" Eleanor asked. "You hardly touched your dinner."

"I'm just tired," Lucy said.

"That's what fresh air and exercise will do for you," Moses said. "Nothing as rewarding as climbing into bed after a busy day."

Lucy smiled. What he said was true. Yet, whether or not she ventured outside, she was always exhausted come nighttime.

"*Gude nacht,*" Lucy said.

"*Gude nacht,*" Moses echoed.

"*Gott segen eich* (God bless you)," Eleanor added.

Lucy left them alone and went up to the bedroom to get ready for bed. It was a chilly night, perfect for tucking in warmly under the covers. She climbed under the heavy quilt, opened the drawer, and removed the Christmas card. She had been desperate to see it again. The room was dim, but she could still make out the wintery scene. Her mind replayed the words on the card in a loop.

Ever since she had opened the envelope, Lucy had felt a nagging feeling that had only grown stronger. As she stared at the small "A" initialed at the bottom of the card, her heart began to race with the possibility that maybe, just maybe, the card was from Albrecht. The more Lucy thought about it, the more she convinced herself it was true. *Suppose he'd written them before he passed?* she reasoned. *What if had arranged to have them to be delivered to me?* After all, she had often told Albrecht how much she loved Christmas and how much she was looking forward to spending their first Christmas together, so what if this was meant to be a surprise?

It all seemed to fit—the scene painted on the front and the words inside. Lucy could see and hear Albrecht in them, and so Lucy decided, in that moment, that Albrecht had sent her the card.

Suddenly, the candle flickered as footsteps approached. Lucy placed the Christmas card back in the drawer and blew out the candle. She pulled the quilt over her body and lay still, staring into the darkness. Lucy had not grown used to the empty bed beside her. She reached over for Albrecht, only to grab a handful of cold sheets. She cried. Then, her hand in her drawer, she reached for the card, a piece of Albrecht, and fell soundly asleep for the first time since Albrecht had died.

Chapter Five: The Bird

The dawn light filtered through the window. Lucy lay still, exhausted from her dream, heart punching against her ribcage to escape. Albrecht had been in her dream. It was summertime and the couple had been in the garden, lying under a large oak tree. Albrecht had laid his head in Lucy's lap. She'd run her fingers through his hair. So vivid was the scene that she could feel his locks. An unusual birdcall had interrupted Lucy's stroking. It had stolen her attention from her beau, causing her to look up into the impossibly thick leafy canopy. She hadn't been able to spot it. *Albrecht would know*, she'd thought. *He knows all the birds*. She'd looked down and he was gone. Panicked, Lucy had jolted up to her feet, calling for her love as though at the top of her lungs. But all that could be heard was the low, mournful call of the hidden bird above. She'd been cold. And damp.

A tear-soaked pillow on a crisp, late autumn morning rudely awakened the young widow. The bird's lonely call echoed in her mind. Seeking comfort, Lucy quickly threw open the bedside drawer and withdrew the card inside. She pressed it to her chest and breathed a sigh of relief.

"You look better this morning," Eleanor said once Lucy had come into the kitchen.

"I slept well," Lucy replied.

Eleanor smiled. Lucy went about her morning tasks. As she kneaded the bread, Eleanor heard Lucy humming. She had never heard Lucy hum before. "Are you sure there is nothing going on?"

Lucy shook her head. Eleanor knew better than most that grief was not a linear process, yet Lucy had not been in good spirits since Albrecht passed. What should have brought relief instead caused suspicion. Eleanor replayed in her mind all that she knew about the girl from the very beginning when she had first heard about Lucy Bontrager, the shopkeeper's daughter.

∞∞∞

Albrecht had lived as if he walked with his head down his whole life, choosing the Fisher's barn as the first place he'd looked up to see the world for the first time. He had stridden into the kitchen, oblivious to his mother sitting in her usual seat, and reached for a glass.

"What's her name?" Eleanor had asked.

Albrecht had whirled around, the glass transformed into a hot potato, the youth's vocabulary reduced to a series of gasps until he, finally, put the glass down. "What are you doing here?"

"It's my house."

"Oh! My! How do you know it's a girl?"

"Believe it or not, I was young once," Eleanor had replied.

Albrecht had smiled, then cupped his neck in his hand, his doe eyes garnishing a lamb-ish grin. "Lucy Bontrager."

Even the way he had said her name was different, his

tongue caressing the words as they left his mouth. He had savored that name, his voice's own guilty pleasure. Eleanor had known then that her son was smitten. For a fortnight, Eleanor had watched Albrecht with his head in the clouds and his feet on the moon. Lucy had been at the heart of it.

Albrecht had been popular in their community, with many of the girls his age hoping he might choose them. However, he had shown little interest in any of them. Eleanor had thought he just hadn't reached the age when women and family interested him. It hadn't occurred to her that he might have been waiting for someone else.

Eleanor smiled presently as she remembered the day of the second *sing*. As usual, the Yoder family had attended church in the morning. Then, that afternoon, Albrecht had spent time with some old friends who had been visiting from out-of-state. Shortly before four o'clock that afternoon, he had come rushing into the kitchen like a rabbit flushed from its hole. He'd narrowly avoided a collision with his mother.

"Albrecht!" Eleanor had chided. "You nearly knocked me over."

"I am sorry, *Maem*," Albrecht had apologized. "I am late for the *sing*."

"There will be others," Eleanor had retorted, oblivious to the significance of the event at hand.

"*Maem*! I can't miss this one. I promised Lucy that I would be there."

Eleanor had smiled. *Ah! Young love,* she'd thought. "Well, you had better hurry, then. You don't want to keep her waiting."

"I've been waiting for her my whole life!" Albrecht had kissed his mother on the cheek before heading upstairs to wash up. Just before heading out of the door, he'd declared, *"Maem*, I am going to marry that girl."

True to his word, Albrecht did marry that girl. The day he brought her home to meet his folks, Eleanor saw why he loved her so much. She was shy but warm. She adored Albrecht, and she was a soothing presence to his more energetic nature. That was all a mother could ask for in a daughter-in-law. Eleanor was pleased to see Albrecht loved.

After the death of Albrecht's brothers, Eleanor and Moses had tried for more children, but God had not willed to give them anymore. Thus, Eleanor was grateful that He had brought Lucy into their lives. She would be her only daughter-in-law. Eleanor had vowed to cherish her.

∞∞∞

"Eleanor! The table is set," Lucy called.

Eleanor basked in the souvenir of her son for a beat before reacting to Lucy. She smiled, then hurried over to fetch the cold meats and bread. Lucy watched the older woman, curiously, wondering where her mind had been just then. Moses came in shortly thereafter. They all sat together to eat.

"Ich saag dank am disch (I offer thanks at the table)," Moses said as he did at the beginning of every meal.

"Ich saag dank am disch," Eleanor and Lucy echoed.

Then they ate. Moses talked about his morning. Lucy was always amazed at how much farmers got done before breakfast was served.

"Don't you think Lucy is looking brighter this morning?"

Eleanor asked.

Moses looked up, studied Lucy's face, and nodded.

Lucy smiled but said nothing. She did feel better that morning, and she knew why. Still, she had decided not to tell Eleanor and Moses about the Christmas card. The debate had raged in her mind as she'd dressed in the morning, but silence was her decided choice of action. Being shy, it was also her easiest. Discovering the card was from Albrecht had brought her much comfort and joy. It might do the same for the Yoders, but if Albrecht had wanted to send his parents a Christmas card, he would have done so. As it was, the envelope only had Lucy's name written on it.

Chapter Six: Every Tear from Their Eyes

T wo days after Lucy received the Christmas card, she went out once more—the fresh air and exercise, along with the surprise gift from Albrecht, having helped her sleep. Upon returning home, the young widow found another envelope waiting for her. Just like the first, the envelope had been placed on the mat outside of the front door. Only her name was written upon it. Lucy opened it immediately. Another winter scene was painted on the front of the card—this time, a group of children with a sled. All were laughing and smiling, enjoying the frozen play land around them. Inside, the card read:

He will wipe every tear from their eyes. There will be no more death or mourning or crying or pain, for the old order of things has passed away.

Lucy read the words silently. A lump formed in her throat. Countless times she had found comfort in those words from the book of Revelation. Now, here they were again. Lucy closed the card and held it to her chest. Tears rolled down her cheeks. She was still. Movement from within the house stirred her from her moment. She quickly regained her composure, hid the card, and proceeded indoors.

"How was your walk?" Eleanor asked. She was seated in the sitting room next to a blazing fire, reaching for her sewing. An old blue-gray cat sat on the mat in front of the fire.

"It was fine," Lucy replied.

Eleanor frowned. "Have you been crying?"

Lucy shook her head. "There is a bit of an icy breeze. It made my eyes water."

"Well, why don't you sit down in front of the fire and warm up."

"*Danki*, but if it's no bother, I wish to lie down in my room."

Eleanor smiled and nodded.

"I'll be down to help with supper," Lucy promised as she left the room.

In her bedroom, Lucy sat upon the bed and re-opened the card. She could scarcely believe that the second could equal the first. However, this latest one was exquisite, its details, perfect. Lucy placed the card on the pillow that had once been Albrecht's, then laid her head down on hers. She pulled the old quilt over her and lay still until she fell asleep.

Dusk was near when Lucy awoke. It had to be close to suppertime. The Christmas card still lay on the pillow beside her. She picked it up, gazed upon it, held it to her breast, then carefully slipped it back into its cream envelope to lay atop the first in her bedside drawer. She headed downstairs.

The cards kept coming though with no discernable pattern or frequency. Three days after the second card had been delivered, a third awaited Lucy upon her return from church with the Yoders. Eleanor stared curiously as Lucy reached for it.

"I think it's from Hannah," Lucy bluffed, "my friend from back home. In her last letter, she said she would send a card."

"How lovely," Eleanor commented.

Lucy was relieved that her mother-in-law did not ask to see it and felt bad for lying. Nevertheless, this was her little Christmas secret. If she was forced to reveal it to her in-laws, the magic would be spoiled.

The next day, Moses and Eleanor were visiting friends when the fourth card arrived. Like the others, it was exquisitely crafted, and the words inside were poignant and meaningful. Lucy carefully placed it with the other cards in the drawer next to her bed. Sitting atop her bed and gazing at the winter outdoors, she thanked the Lord for the blessing that these cards had been. Lucy had not looked forward to anything since Albrecht's death. Each day, she had been going through the motions so that Eleanor and Moses would not worry about her. Yet, she lived without living. There was no joy or pleasure in life after losing Albrecht. Now, the anticipation of receiving the Christmas cards made it easy for Lucy to get out of bed in the morning. It made her look forward to the day ahead. It was pleasant to feel normal again and to feel loved once more, for each card was further proof that Albrecht had organized the cards for her because he knew her well and knew what she needed to hear.

Chapter Seven: The Dogwood Tree

Two weeks had passed since Lucy received the first Christmas card, and the weather had yet to yield a snowfall. It was the middle of December and brutally cold. The lack of snow worried Moses, who as a farmer, was suspicious of unusual weather patterns and what it might mean for the year ahead.

"*Gott* will bring the snow when He sees fit," Eleanor reminded her better half as he grumbled over his breakfast porridge.

"Well, let's hope He brings it soon," Moses replied. "We need that snow to fill our rivers and dams come springtime."

"Everything happens in His time," Eleanor reminded him, gently.

Moses nodded. Nothing more was said. Lucy stared out of the window, her breakfast untouched and her coffee growing cold. Eleanor frowned. Lucy had been better over the last two weeks, as though something had kick-started her will to live. However, it now seemed as though she were retreating into herself again.

"Lucy?" Eleanor asked. "Are you all right?"

Lucy did not budge. Eleanor was unsure if she had heard her. She reached out her hand and placed it over Lucy's, startling the latter.

"I'm sorry," Eleanor apologized. "I just wanted to see if you were quite well."

Lucy nodded but looked strained.

"Are you sure?" Eleanor asked.

"Leave the poor girl alone, Eleanor," Moses instructed. "You're as bad as those hens in the barn, pecking away at each other."

Eleanor sighed and sat back in her seat. She took a sip of coffee to collect her thoughts. However, with her husband's rebuke still ringing in her ears, she said nothing more.

Lucy picked up her spoon and took a mouthful of the porridge. It had grown cold, sticking to her palate like glue. She quickly took a sip of coffee to wash it down. Its lukewarm temperature was not what she had expected. She choked and coughed.

"I'm all right," Lucy insisted. "I just need a sip of water." She walked over to the sink and took a glass off the drying rack. She poured some water and took a sip. She could feel Eleanor and Moses's eyes on the back of her head. Lucy heard a chair scraping against the wooden floorboards. She turned to see Moses getting up from the table. Lucy rinsed the glass and placed it back onto the drying rack.

"*Danki* for breakfast," Moses said.

Eleanor smiled at him. Moses headed out the back door while Lucy began to gather the breakfast dishes.

"I am going into town this morning," Eleanor said, "to visit with Mrs. Stoltzfus. Would you like to come with me?"

"Would you mind if I didn't?" Lucy asked. "I am not really feeling up to a walk into town, and if I stay here, I can prepare lunch for Moses and do whatever chores need tending to."

"Are you sure?" Eleanor asked. "It might be nice to get out of the house and see some friendly faces. You must get so tired of only talking to us."

"Not at all," Lucy reassured her.

"Very well," Eleanor said, trying, in vain, to hide the disappointment in her voice. "If you say so."

After Eleanor had left for town, Lucy did the few chores that remained and then headed upstairs to her bedroom. She sat on the edge of the bed, opened the small bedside drawer, and removed the Christmas cards. There were six in total. She had expected one to come the day before despite their random deliveries. When it had not, she'd felt depressed. Furthermore, her reaction embarrassed her, making it more difficult to hide from her in-laws. Cards in hand coupled with the prospect of never receiving another, an unbearable sadness descended upon her, slouching her shoulders and pressing down upon her chest. She had not felt this way since Moses had come stumbling up the driveway with his son in his arms, tears streaming down his dusty cheeks.

∞∞∞

It had been a hot and balmy day in late August. Lucy had been irritable. She'd spent most of the day moving from window to window looking for a breeze, but the air had been heavy, stagnant.

"It's much too hot to eat," Eleanor had remarked at lunchtime. "I think cold meats and fruit will suffice."

40

Lucy had not argued. She'd helped her mother-in-law prepare a simple meal. Albrecht had entered from tending the fields, tanned and perspiring, his old straw hat hanging off his head. Upon making eye contact with his bride, he'd broken into a goofy grin, like a teenage boy when he gets his crush's attention for the first time.

"Whew! It is hot out there today."

"Here." Lucy had handed him a glass of cool lemonade.

"I don't think I've loved you more," Albrecht had declared, taking the glass from her hand.

"Where is your *daed*?" Eleanor had asked.

"Jakob forgot to fill the calf's water trough again," Albrecht had answered. "So, he is having a word with the help."

Eleanor had sighed. "I swear that boy would forget to show up at his own funeral!"

Albrecht had giggled, eyes ever on his bride, sipping his drink. "I need to go into town after lunch."

"What for?" Eleanor had asked.

"*Daed* says that Mr. Beiler at the farm shop has got something new to help treat the pests," Albrecht had explained. "We need it. All the rain had those little pests multiply such that they are driving the animals mad." Albrecht had turned to look at Lucy. "You fancy taking a trip into town with me?"

Lucy had shaken her head. "It's much too hot to be sitting in a buggy."

"Very well. I think I'll just take the horse into town. It'll be quicker, and I might just feel a breeze through my hair."

Lucy had glanced at Albrecht. Her stomach had fluttered. The boy had been able to make her feel multiple emotions at once, but they all made her love him more. This had happened virtually every time their eyes had met.

Moses had arrived, hot and bothered. No one asked him what was wrong, and he did not offer to explain his mood. Instead, they'd all eaten the buffet of cold meats and fruit before Albrecht had excused himself. Lucy had quickly cleaned up to join her husband upstairs. She had caught him shirtless, just in time for some eye candy.

"Are you sure that I can't convince you to come with me?" Albrecht had asked as he splashed water on his face. Some drops had fallen to his chest, so Lucy'd had an excuse to brush her hands against his farmer's pecs.

"It is much too hot."

Albrecht had thought she was talking about the weather. With a warm smile, the happy groom had reached out his hand for Lucy's. Their fingers had interlaced. He'd pulled her into himself where she'd fit perfectly under his chin. "I love you," he had said, simply.

"I love you too," Lucy had replied.

They had remained so for an indeterminate amount of time; for to youths in love, eternity in each other's arms is too short of a time. Lucy had listened to Albrecht's gentle heartbeat, lulled into joyous bliss, resting in the arms of love.

"I'd better be going," Albrecht had said, flatly.

Lucy had looked up at him, and he had leaned down to kiss her. She'd returned her head onto his chest. "Just one more minute."

His giggle was the last thing Lucy had ever heard from Albrecht. He'd gently pushed her away from him by her shoulders, gazed at her longingly, and kissed her on the forehead. He'd buttoned up his shirt and left her life for good.

When dinnertime had arrived on the fateful day, Lucy had waited on the front porch. The heat had dulled the senses, and the humidity had been oppressive all day. The young bride had struggled to breathe. She'd clutched the banister so tightly that her knuckles were white.

"Are they back yet?" Eleanor had called from within the house.

"*Nee*," had been Lucy's reply.

Eleanor had sighed about as loudly as she sneezed. Only she could let you know her disappointment from the basement as you rummaged in the attic. Moses wisely stayed out of earshot in the fields from dawn 'til dusk, save for his meals.

Albrecht had been due to return earlier. Moses had set off to find him, a task that should not have taken as long as it had. Neither of them had returned.

"His horse probably threw a shoe," Eleanor had tried to be reassuring as worrying mothers do when they try to hide their panic.

Lucy had seen a figure in the distance. She had squinted in the hopes of recognizing who it was. It was a man, heavy laden, carrying something in his arms. "Someone's here!" Lucy had corrected her previous answer.

"What was that, *Liewi*?" Eleanor had asked, joining her daughter-in-law on the porch.

Lucy had stood frozen in the hot weather. Eleanor's screech had pierced the twilight. A flock of birds had all flown off from a nearby dogwood tree, making haste away from the night hound on the Yoder porch. Lucy had closed her eyes, disbelieving. Pathetically, she'd reasoned that, if she didn't see Albrecht in his father's arms, he would be fine. Bargaining with grief renders us all fools.

Moses had walked a bride's pace to the Yoder front porch, the crickets playing their eerie music, father taking his son away from his bride as he escorted him to the grave. His tear-soaked, dusty cheeks were what had convinced Lucy that the worst was true. She had collapsed to her knees—the floor beneath her a puddle of tears—and opened her mouth for air. Then, her soul had wailed, crying out from the cavernous depths of her being to beckon back to her side her dearly departed. The crickets had ceased their tune. The bats had halted their exit from the barn as though letting the farm boy's soul pass them by on his way to the Father. Not a hoof beat nor a rustle nor peep nor hoot could be heard on the Yoder homestead. Instead, the echoes of Lucy's and Eleanor's sobs had set the sun into the night sky. Then, the lambs had bleated, the cattle had groaned, and the rooster had crowed, all of Albrecht's friends bidding him farewell into the night.

Lucy had made her way to the remains of her beloved, knelt beside him, and taken his hand in hers. It had been cold, lifeless, and heavy, so unlike the hand she had always known. The unfamiliarity had repulsed her such that she had drawn her hand back to herself. Upon gazing at Albrecht's face, however, she had wept, folding herself over onto his chest. Her wails had extinguished the sun's last rays. Dusk passed. Night was ushered in to the young widow's wails.

Moses had then spoken. "I brought our *buwe* home. They told me to leave him, but I couldn't leave him on the road." He had sobbed as he had lain Albrecht's broken remains on the porch. Eleanor had crumpled over he who had been her only remaining child. She'd mourned his loss, his brothers, and the end of their lineage.

"What happened?" Eleanor had asked.

Moses had shaken his head as he had struggled to find the words. He had sniffled, sobbed, and forced himself to say, "He was thrown from the horse. It was Mr. Lapp who found him. Maybe it was the copperheads because of the heat. Maybe the horse got spooked."

Moses' words had taken Lucy's breath away. *That's it?* she had thought. *Just a snake scaring a horse? That's all it took to make me a widow? Albrecht is dead because of that?* She'd raised her head off Albrecht's chest.

Eleanor had then taken Lucy's place. Primal sobs had reverberated from the cavernous deep within the dark recesses of a mother's soul who had outlived all her offspring. Crickets had held their song. Lucy had held her tongue, for any remark before such grief would seem pithy. Only one other soul in the universe could empathize dredging sorrow's abyss.

Softly, tenderly, Moses had said, "The doctor's on his way. Come inside. Come on." He'd then lifted his bride off Albrecht's remains and carried her across the threshold.

Lucy had not followed. She had remained on the porch, clutching Albrecht's arm. "You promised that you would come back to me," she had whimpered. "You promised." She had awaited a reply. When none was forthcoming, she had lain her head upon his chest, where, only hours earlier, she had heard his heartbeat. Hollow silence had filled the air.

Lucy's recollection of the events between Albrecht's death and funeral were akin to cyphering a mosaic with missing tiles or a stained-glassed window with missing pieces. She couldn't be sure of the chronology, either. The words *broken neck*, Albrecht's horse returning, a mumbled prayer with the bishop in the Yoder sitting room, her beloved in a casket, a pair of fingers pressing for a pulse, Albrecht's horse grazing in a neighboring paddock, were images she could recall when she had been drunk with grief. How her hangover had ended, however, was etched in her mind.

Lucy had entered the kitchen one afternoon shortly after Albrecht had been buried. She'd frozen. *Something's missing,* she'd thought. There, around the kitchen table, only three chairs had stood. "Albrecht's chair! Where is Albrecht's chair?" The young widow had been near hysteria.

Both Moses and Eleanor had been seated at the kitchen table, and they had both gazed at her tenderly.

"Where is it?" Lucy had repeated.

Eleanor had looked to Moses, who had sighed and risen from his chair. "Come."

The pair had walked out of the back door, away from the house, past the barn, through a meadow to an ancient dogwood tree. An old wooden swing hung from the thickest branch.

"There," Moses had said, pointing to a wooden cross in the ground flanked by two other weathered crosses.

Lucy had frowned.

"We did it when Isaac and Elijah died," Moses had explained. "Eleanor wanted a place on the farm where she could come to remember her boys. I used their kitchen chairs to create a memorial. When they were all...together"—his voice had cracked—"this place was their favorite spot." He had pressed his tongue against his teeth and tilted his head upward. Nevertheless, the tears could not be stopped. His voice had pitched higher as he sobbed, "So, we like to come here when we miss them."

Lucy had walked up to the newest cross and touched the polished wood. She'd felt her throat swell as she blinked back tears. "Albrecht never brought me here."

"Albrecht was never one to live in the past," Moses had sniffled. "This was for Eleanor."

Lucy had nodded. Albrecht had not told her much about his brothers, other than how they had died. She had not pried. "I am sorry for my outburst in the kitchen. When I saw the missing chair, I assumed..." Her voice had trailed off.

"That we had put it away," Moses had finished. "Having an empty seat at the table is a constant reminder of our loss. At least now the chair has a new purpose. It marks Albrecht's place on the farm and in our hearts, forever." Moses had looked to his daughter-in-law and said, "I should be getting back."

"Do you mind if I stay a while?" Lucy had asked.

"Stay as long as you like."

Moses had then left. Once he had been out of sight, Lucy had sat upon the swing. She had closed her eyes and imagined Albrecht and his older brothers playing there as children. Giggles, arguments over whose turn it was on the swing, boys running around, were all she could manage. It had been hard to picture Albrecht as a boy. Lucy had hoped that she and Albrecht might have their own children one day and then she would see Albrecht's features in a small child. She'd then imagined a future that was lost, one in which her sons played with Albrecht under the same dogwood tree.

The cry of a kestrel from above had evaporated Lucy's fantasy. Indeed, what was the point of imagining children playing around a memorial? Her longing had caused pain in the pit of her stomach. She had risen and made haste toward the house in order to ease her pain. She knew that she would never come back to that place. It was too painful to imagine what might have been.

As Lucy sat atop the bed that she had once shared with Albrecht, clutching the Christmas cards, she was thrust back into the present to mourn anew. A knock at the door caused Lucy to jump up to her feet and drop the cards.

"Lucy?" Eleanor opened the door. "Are you all right?"

"Fine," Lucy mumbled.

"How long have you been in here?"

Lucy shrugged. "What time is it?"

"A little after three."

"Oh no!" Lucy exclaimed. "I forgot all about lunch."

"Don't worry," Eleanor soothed. "Moses is a grown man; he is perfectly capable of making a sandwich."

"I am so sorry, Eleanor. I came in here for a quick lie down, and I must have fallen asleep."

"Please, don't worry yourself, *Liewi*. I am sorry to disturb you, but I found this on the mat outside when I returned home."

Lucy then spotted the cream envelope in Eleanor's hand. She kicked herself for not having noticed it sooner. Her mad scramble to wrench it from her mother-in-law's hand startled them both. Eleanor backed away.

"Is it another card from your friend, Hannah?" Eleanor asked.

"Yes," Lucy lied. "She is just full of the *Grischtdaag* spirit."

Eleanor smiled. "Come downstairs when you are ready," she said and left the room.

Lucy clutched the envelope to her chest and relaxed for the first time in days.

Chapter Eight: Confession

Lucy opened the envelope. A single, lifelike snowflake had been painted on the cover. Lucy touched it, expecting it to be cold. Then she feared it would melt, such was its mesmerizing effect. Inside the card was a quote about the tiny miracles of snowflakes. *What a way to describe them!* she thought. It reminded her of a conversation she had had with Albrecht on their first buggy ride together.

"Have you ever considered that life is a series of small miracles?" Albrecht had asked.

"How so?" Lucy had wondered.

"Just look around us. Every blade of grass and every flower petal is a small miracle. The eyelashes that brush your cheeks are small miracles. It is our privilege to appreciate them. For example, I appreciate walking through the barn doors to lay my eyes upon you. I appreciate seeing you standing opposite the table from me, singing, smiling—especially the smiling!—and clasping your hands across your chest when you sing. I appreciate your long eyelashes. I appreciate your voice."

"That's a lot of appreciation," Lucy had remarked.

Smiling wryly, Albrecht had replied, "Well, there is a lot in life to be thankful for."

Aware of her chores, Lucy paused her nostalgia and headed

to the kitchen to scrub the floors. She felt obliged to her in-laws for having slept through lunch. Upon her hands and knees, she scrubbed, placed her sponge in the bucket, and repeated.

"Lucy?" Eleanor called. "Can you come here, please?"

Lucy arose and went to her mother-in-law. She walked quickly to the sitting room, but Eleanor was not there. Lucy went up the stairs to the master bedroom, but Eleanor was not there, either.

"Lucy?" Eleanor called anew.

This time, Lucy realized that she was calling from her bedroom. Eleanor was standing next to Lucy's bed. In her hand, she was holding one of the Christmas cards.

"Where did you find that?" Lucy asked.

"I was just collecting the carpets to dust, and I found it under the bed," Eleanor explained.

Lucy frowned. She must have left one on the floor when they had fallen.

"This card isn't from your friend Hannah, is it?" she asked.

Lucy said nothing.

"I did think it was strange that you did not want to display it on the mantelpiece," Eleanor continued. "Can you tell me who sent it to you?"

"I don't know," Lucy admitted.

Eleanor frowned. "You don't know?"

Lucy shook her head. "They have just been arriving on the porch."

"They?"

Lucy opened the drawer to her nightstand, removed the small stack of cards, and handed them to Eleanor. The latter inspected them, quietly. Lucy watched her face, trying to determine her reaction, but Eleanor was poker-faced. Once she had inspected the last card, she handed them all back to Lucy.

"You really have no idea who is sending these cards to you?"

Lucy was unsure whether to tell Eleanor of her theory. She did not want her mother-in-law to think she was mad with grief or ill. On the other hand, it would be nice to test out her theory and ask Eleanor to weigh in on the subject. "I have an idea of who's been sending them."

"Who?" Eleanor asked.

Lucy exhaled slowly before answering. "I think it might be Albrecht."

Eleanor's face paled. "What do you mean?"

"I am not crazy," Lucy said. "I know that Albrecht is not here anymore. But when he was alive, we spoke a lot about *Grischtdaag* and how much we were looking forward to it, and maybe he organized for the cards to be delivered before he died."

Eleanor cocked her head to the side. Lucy looked down at her hands and puffed her cheeks. Eleanor was mute. It was obvious that Lucy had an interested suitor. Her frown softened. She looked upon her youngest son's beloved with compassion.

"Lucy," Eleanor said, softly.

"Wait!" Lucy insisted. "Just look at some of the things that are written inside. How could anyone have known just the right thing to say? Whoever is writing these cards knows me and knows what I want to hear."

"How certain can you be that someone from your *gmay* didn't send these to you?" Eleanor asked.

"They didn't," Lucy said.

"And how do you know?"

"I just do," Lucy said stubbornly.

Eleanor looked down at the cards in her hand. Her heart was heavy. Her instinct was to protect Lucy, but not in a fantasy. Eleanor knew how difficult it was to move on. She was an old hand at it. Lucy was young and needed to learn to let go. Albrecht was with God and had been since the moment he died. Eleanor knew that if Lucy believed she was receiving messages from Albrecht, she would never be able to let him go and move forward with her life.

"I am sorry, Lucy," Eleanor said, handing her the pile of cards. "I know how much you want these to be from Albrecht, but I don't believe that he sent you these *Grischtdaag* cards."

Lucy frowned. Eleanor moved to exit the room. Lucy expected more.

"But how do you know?" Lucy asked. "He could have written them before he died."

Eleanor shook her head. "It's not that. We raised Albrecht to see art and artistic expression as the *Ordnung* prescribes. He would never have created art that wasn't functional in some way, not even as a celebration of *Grischtdaag*."

"But he may have changed his mind," Lucy argued. "Albrecht had a beautiful mind."

Eleanor pitied Lucy. She placed a hand on the widow's cheek. "He did, but he expressed himself through his words. We don't believe in beauty without purpose, and Albrecht always spoke with purpose. Even if Albrecht did change his belief about art, I still don't think that these cards are from him."

"How can you be so sure?"

"Because Albrecht was *gut* at many things, but he was chaotic and messy. When he was a *buwe*, I received countless letters from his teacher about the state of his handwriting, and no matter how much he tried, he was never orderly. It's not his handwriting," Eleanor concluded, gently.

Lucy felt hollow. Her fantasy was now burst, and she felt silly. How could she have clung to the notion that her dead husband had sent her Christmas cards? The embarrassment was more than she could bear. "I am a fool," she whispered.

"*Nee,*" Eleanor said. "You are not a fool."

"I am," Lucy said, suddenly feeling angry. "I was so convinced that Albrecht sent me these cards that I didn't see what was right in front of me. When Albrecht and I first started going out, he sent me letters. I know what his handwriting looks like, but I was just so desperate to believe he was still with me that I was blind to everything else. How could I have been so stupid?" She wept. Her tears were absorbed by the cards pressed against her chest.

"I am sorry, Lucy," Eleanor said. "I know how much you wanted these cards to be from Albrecht, but he is gone, and the only part of him left is the part of him you carry in your heart."

Lucy collapsed onto the bed. "I should have told you sooner about the cards."

"Why didn't you?" Eleanor asked.

Lucy did not answer right away. "Because I thought that it would spoil their magic."

"And you were right," Eleanor said.

Lucy sniffled and gesticulated, not knowing if she should throw the cards down, wipe her nose, or cry on Eleanor's shoulder. "Who's sending them?" she asked. "If it's not Albrecht, then who is sending me these cards?"

Eleanor shook her head. "I don't know."

"What do they want?"

Eleanor did not have an answer. She, too, was perplexed by the mysterious sender and what exactly the Christmas cards meant. "We need to find out."

Chapter Nine: A Reason

"**L**ucy," Moses called out.

The widow looked up from her plate. Her thin face was pale and drawn. She had aged. Moses was not a man of many words; he chose his carefully. Seeing that Lucy was hurt and that the Christmas cards she had received had left her puzzled—and concluding that Lucy did not need any more pain—Moses had decided to find the person who had sent her the cards. That way, she would have answers and closure.

"If you want to know who sent you these *Grischtdaag* cards, then you should find out."

Eleanor looked across at her husband, bemused. She had told Moses all about the mysterious cards, and they had both agreed that it would be best to just forget about them and move on. She now worried that if Lucy went looking for answers, there may be no end to her grief. It was nothing certain that closure would be found once the mystery of the sender was solved. While Moses had agreed, he had been unable to sleep.

"Only if you want to," Eleanor interjected.

Moses nodded.

"Do you think that I should?" Lucy asked, looking from Moses to Eleanor.

"I think there is a reason that someone chose to send you

the cards," Moses said. "For a while, they made you happy again. If I were in your shoes, I'd want to know who sent them and why."

Indeed, the Christmas cards had made Lucy happy, and it had not just been because she'd thought they were from Albrecht. It had also been the way the cards were crafted and the careful choice of words written inside. Still, she was grieving her fantasy as well as Albrecht. A wild goose chase may only lead to added mourning. Not catching the goose was unthinkable. *Perhaps it may be better to just put the cards behind me and move on?* she thought.

"I'm not sure I want to know who sent them," Lucy confessed.

Moses nodded. No more was said on the matter.

For the rest of the day, Lucy busied herself with the household chores, hoping to forget the Christmas cards. It did not work. She could not understand the intention behind sending them, nor why the sender chose to remain anonymous. By the time supper arrived, Lucy had changed her mind. She needed to know who had sent them and why.

"I do want to find out," Lucy declared.

Moses and Eleanor looked surprised.

"Although, I'm not sure how to go about such a task."

Moses thought for a moment. "It shouldn't be too difficult. Someone is obviously delivering the cards. All you need to do is wait for another card to be delivered. It's either him or someone he knows."

"But they are never delivered at the same time or on consecutive days," Lucy said.

"Well, it may be a bit of a waiting game," Moses said. "I have faith that you can find out if you are determined to do so."

Lucy nodded. She was determined to find out who was sending the cards. A little while later, she finished supper, washed the dishes, and packed everything away. She then made her way to the sitting room. As she approached, she heard Moses and Eleanor talking in hard whispers.

"I don't think it's a *gut* idea," Eleanor said. "What if she gets hurt again?"

"She's stronger than you give her credit for," Moses replied.

"But what *gut* can come of finding the sender?" Eleanor asked.

"If someone was sending you *Grischtdaag* cards with words of comfort and hope, would you not wish to know who was sending them and what encouraged them to do so?"

The room was quiet for a few moments, and Lucy took Eleanor's silence to mean that she agreed with Moses.

"I know that you just want to protect her," Moses said, "but she will be fine."

Lucy heard footsteps and hurried back down the hallway toward the kitchen.

"Lucy? Do you need any help?" Eleanor called.

"*Nee*," Lucy replied. "It's all done."

"*Gut*. Then come to the sitting room. Moses is going to read from the Bible."

Chapter Ten: The Card Bearer

No cards were delivered for three days, frustrating Lucy's spying efforts. Once she had made the decision to discover the identity of the mysterious Christmas card sender, the cards had stopped coming. Perhaps no more would come and she would never learn who had sent them to her.

Lucy took her usual spot at the window on the fourth day. The ledge of the front room window was not a particularly comfortable spot, but it gave her the best view of the porch and the road in front of the house. Previously, Lucy had only found the cards in the afternoon, so she had developed a routine whereby she'd do her chores before midday, take up her residence at the window, and have lunch delivered to her in the front room. Eleanor's doubts about the endeavor grew with each passing day. She would deliver the lunch sandwich, look concerned, then purse her lips as though hinting to Lucy that she should give up without making it seem that she was pulling the plug. After all, Eleanor did not wish to cross Moses. To exacerbate the situation was the Amish belief that idleness is a sin. Lucy felt guilty as the minutes rolled into hours and she did nothing but stare out the window. She prayed to God for understanding that her actions had purpose and for forgiveness if He disagreed.

Just before three o'clock on the fourth day, the pale blue sky grew congested with thick, gray clouds, like smog during rush hour. They then grew darker. Moses' prediction that there would be bad weather was about to come true. The threat of a blizzard only added to Lucy's worries. Such adverse weather would discourage any delivery on the day, and she would be no closer to solving the mystery.

Yet, as she stared out at the far hills, she suddenly heard the small wrought-iron gate at the bottom of the Yoder yard squeak. Lucy turned to get a better look. A young boy came up the front path. He was skulking, shifting his gaze as though he knew he was about to do something he wasn't supposed to do. Lucy stood up and shielded herself behind the sheer under-curtain so as to remain unseen. The boy climbed up the porch steps. She was amazed at how quiet he was. He reached into his coat and pulled out a cream envelope, which he then deposited onto the door-mat. Seizing her chance, Lucy scurried away from the window and to the front door. She threw it open with such force that the little boy was frozen to the spot. They stared at each other. In a blink, though, the little boy was gone.

"Wait!" Lucy cried. She raced barefoot after the boy. Her calves burned as she tore after him. It was like chasing a jackrabbit. The boy reached the gate, opened it, and disappeared down the road. Moses appeared from around the house a moment later looking surprised.

"It's him," Lucy said, panting. "He delivered the *Grischtdaag* card."

Moses frowned, looking down the road where the boy had disappeared. "Are you sure?" he asked, sounding uncertain.

"*Ya,*" Lucy replied. "I saw him. He placed the card on the

mat."

Moses was still frowning.

"Who is he?" Lucy asked.

"His name is Noah Lehman," Moses said. "He is a farmhand at the Peachey farm just down the road."

"Peachey" seemed familiar to Lucy, but she couldn't quite remember where she had heard it before.

"I know that name, but I'm not sure why," Lucy admitted.

"The farm is owned by Jacob Peachey," he explained. "They have a son, Andy."

"How old is Andy?" Lucy asked.

Moses did not answer right away. Something was bothering him.

"Moses?" Lucy said.

"Andy is the same age as Albrecht," Moses said. "They used to be best friends."

What Moses was telling Lucy then clicked into place. The initial at the bottom of the cards belonged to Andy. He was the one sending her the cards and having his farmhand deliver them. What Lucy did not know was why Albrecht's old friend would send her Christmas cards.

Part Two

Chapter One: The Widow

"**A**ndy?" Sarah Peachey called out. A tall woman with a kindly face and portly figure appeared in the doorway. "Lunch is ready."

Andy Peachey had been shoveling hay in the barn since morning on one of the hottest days of the year. He wiped the sweat off his brow and walked over to the barn doors, hoping to catch a breeze for a moment's respite from the stifling heat. He faced the house.

"Coming."

Andy rested the pitchfork against the wooden wall of the barn and walked over to a pail of water. He dipped both hands inside and splashed water onto his face and neck. The water was warm, yet it was better than sweat. Andy repeated the gesture thrice more. Once finished, he left the barn and walked toward the farmhouse to join his parents for lunch.

The back door was open. Andy could hear his parents speaking quietly between themselves. "It's such a tragedy," Sarah said, shaking her head. "And that poor—" Her voice trailed off once she spotted Andy in the doorway. "Come, sit," she said. "I made lemonade. You must be thirsty."

"What were you talking about?" Andy asked his mother.

Jacob Peachey and Sarah looked to each other, then lowered

their eyes. Neither responded.

"Tell me," Andy insisted.

"There was an accident yesterday," Jacob explained, "on the road outside of the King farm."

"Was anyone hurt?" Andy asked. His parents acted as before. He frowned. "What happened?"

Jacob sighed, shifting in his chair. "Albrecht Yoder was thrown from his horse," Jacob said. "They think maybe the horse was startled by a copperhead."

Andy was dizzy. "Is he all right?"

Jacob shook his head. "*Nee*. He broke his neck."

Andy struggled to breathe.

Sarah shook her head as though that would make her tears retreat back into her eyes. "Poor Moses and Eleanor," was all that she could manage.

"It's a tragedy," Jacob agreed.

Andy was mute, the news sucking the air and the appetite out of him. His childhood friend—best friend until their differences separated them—was now dead. They had been inseparable. As they grew older, however, their interests and opinions changed, leading them down different paths. There had never been bad blood between them; they just simply stopped being friends. Andy had considered reaching out to Albrecht after his diagnosis, but he never did.

"I cannot stop thinking about his poor *fraa*," Sarah said. "They've only been married for a few months!"

Albrecht had gotten married at the beginning of the year, not long ago. Andy was supposed to have gone to the wedding, but he had been in the hospital. His doctor had thought he might be suitable for an experimental trial to correct his ailment, but his condition was too advanced. Thus, he missed out on the wedding and the treatment.

Collecting herself, Sarah's practical side kicked in. "I will prepare food for the Yoders this afternoon. Andy can deliver it."

"Me?"

"*Ya.* You know the Yoders better than any of us."

"I haven't seen them for years," Andy protested.

"Still, they were always kind to you. You *will* go and show your respect," Jacob interjected.

Andy nodded.

Late in the afternoon, Andy had carried a basket of food to the Yoder farm. His mother had agonized over what to send, having settled on potato salad, a loaf of cornbread, a jar of pickled onions, and some preserves. Andy had knocked, and Eleanor Yoder opened the door, wearing black and a grief-stricken smile.

"*Gude daag,* Andy," she'd said.

"*Gude daag,* Mrs. Yoder," Andy had replied. "My *maem* sent some food." He'd thrust the basket forward.

"*Danki,*" Eleanor had managed.

Andy had been unsure what to say next. Those at his grandfather's funeral had smiled stoically, looking hardly sentimental. He'd felt that it was inappropriate at this time, given his friendship with Albrecht. He'd smiled, then stopped himself. From Eleanor's view, Andy had grimaced. His face had turned to surprise once he spotted a young woman in the hallway behind Mrs. Yoder. She, too, was wearing black. Andy had deduced that it was Albrecht's widow. She'd caught his eye but hadn't engaged.

"Will we see you at the funeral?"

"*Ya,* Mrs. Yoder," Andy had promised. "We will all be there."

He was back to his senses. Before turning away, he'd taken one last look at Lucy. The look in her eyes had haunted him all the way home and ever since. It was the portrait of pain, the painting of grief, the look of a widow. He had to do something.

Chapter Two: The Funeral

Three days after Albrecht Yoder had died, the community was invited to the Yoders' barn for the funeral. Andy had only ever been to his grandfather's funeral before. The memory of that day was still fresh in his mind, ten years later.

On the morning of the funeral, Andy finished his chores on the farm, then returned home to change into a black jacket and matching trousers. The Peachey family then walked to the Yoder farm. Others arrived in buggies. Andy spotted Bishop Fisher standing outside of the barn. He looked around for Albrecht's widow, but she was nowhere to be seen. The look he had seen on her face haunted him anew.

"Come, Andy, hurry," Sarah Peachey urged. "It's almost time."

People filed into the barn. At one end of the space lay Albrecht's remains, while the people sat on benches to face him.

"*Gude mariye*," Bishop Fisher said.

There were murmurs from the community.

"On behalf of the Yoder family, I would like to express our gratitude for your coming today."

Andy craned his neck to catch sight of the Yoders. He still could not see the widow.

"Let us begin with the hymn "Jesus My Shepherd.""

Upon singing the song from the *Ausbund*, Bishop Fisher cleared his throat and began. Andy listened, his attention divided between the homily and Lucy Yoder's ghostly grieving mien from when he'd delivered the basket of food. He closed his eyes to concentrate on the bishop.

The congregation rose and began to sing.

"Andy! Stand up," Sarah exhorted.

Closing his eyes had only caused him to concentrate more on Lucy. Andy hurried to his feet. Once the hymn was over and all had regained their seats, the bishop told the creation story, then invited the men attending the casket to the front of the room. One of the men was Albrecht's father, Moses, but Andy did not recognize the others. *Perhaps they are cousins*, he thought.

Moses gave his son one last affectionate look before closing the lid of the casket on his youngest child. The pallbearers each lifted the casket and carried it out from the barn into the sunlight. Mother Nature, it seemed, was not mourning that day. The mournful followed. The casket was loaded onto the hearse buggy. It led the way up a dirt road to the cemetery. All followed. None spoke. Bishop Fisher took his place at the top of the grave while all others gathered 'round. Finally, Andy caught sight of Lucy Yoder. She was poker-faced as though she wore a mask, still and unmoving.

"Let us pray," Bishop Fisher announced. All bowed their heads and prayed in silence. Then, the bishop thanked everyone for coming. It was over. The crowd dispersed. Andy looked for Lucy. She was not with her in-laws, nor was she at the side of the grave.

"Andy, are you coming?" Sarah asked.

Andy spotted Lucy standing next to a large silver maple tree, her back turned to him. "I'll be right there," Andy promised his mother. He walked toward Lucy, having no idea what to say, possessed only by the conviction that something needed to be said. Lucy heard him approach and turned to face him but held her tongue.

"*Gude daag*," Andy said.

Lucy turned away from him, distracted. "What is that?"

Andy frowned. He could not see what she was talking about, so he listened carefully. There was a soft coo. "It's a mourning dove," he declared.

Lucy chuffed. "It seems fitting."

Neither spoke, listening instead to the mourning dove's song. Lucy turned around and left. Andy stayed under the silver maple, contemplating Lucy's silhouette. Jacob Peachey cleared his throat. It was time for Andy to go.

The Peacheys made their way home in silence, the dove's call still echoing through the woods and the meadows. Andy was preoccupied with Lucy. He was puzzled by his attraction to her despite having never met her before. He was drawn to her, compelled to comfort her. How he could help appropriately was another matter.

Chapter Three: The Backyard Birder

Andy Peachey sat on his porch in an old wooden rocking chair. He did not rock the chair because he knew that it would disturb the birds, so instead, he sat still, perched as if he were a bird himself.

Several months had passed since Andy had first laid eyes on Lucy Yoder. The birds of the summer, the Yellow Warblers, American Woodcocks, and sparrows would soon fly south, leaving only the winter birds behind. Andy was looking forward to hearing the gentle cheeping of the Downy Woodpecker or shrill whistle of the Cedar Waxwing once again. Andy had been a keen birder since he was out of diapers. In fact, it had accelerated his training. His love of birds had come from his grandfather. He had been a man who had spent every free moment outside with his gaze toward the heavens. Grandfather had promised to grandson that if he learned to use the pot, he'd take him away from the porch and into the woods for birdwatching. Andy had learned in record time.

Old man Peachey had been afflicted with macular degeneration at the age of sixty, and by the time he was seventy years old, he was completely blind. Yet his blindness had never stopped him from doing what he loved. "You don't have to be able to see them to appreciate their beauty," he had once said.

"Just listen to their call, and let your imagination paint the picture for you."

Andy sat on an old rocker thinking about his grandfather. While it had been years since he'd passed, Andy had not grown accustomed to his loss. Old man Peachey had been generous with his love and his wisdom. How Andy could use that wisdom now!

"Andy?"

"I'm outside, *Maem*," Andy replied.

"Lunch is ready," she said.

Andy nodded. His mother returned to her duties.

A small bird landed on a tree branch at the bottom of the garden. Andy waited for it to call. His field of vision had quickly eroded since the winter; he was no longer able to see details beyond the porch clearly. Andy had suffered from middle onset macular degeneration since the age of fifteen. His love of birds had been a gift from his grandfather; his disease, a curse. He, too, would go blind.

The bird teased Andy, remaining mute yet turning its head this way and that in search of food and cyphering threats from the benign. Without its song, Andy would be unable to paint a mental picture. Andy leaned on the arms of the chair to pull himself up. The sudden motion startled the bird, and it flew off. Andy sighed, walked slowly toward the front door, pulled open the screen door, which squeaked its displeasure at being disturbed, and headed indoors.

Sarah Peachey placed lunch on the table as Andy entered the dining room. His father was already seated. He looked up at his son as he came in, not to look at him but to see if his son could see. Unlike his father, Andy's skin was pale, not tanned and weathered. "The frosted Amish boy," was his nickname. His fingernails were clean, and his clothes were rarely soiled with sweat from work on the farm.

"Sit, Andy," Sarah instructed.

Andy took his place across the table from his father. He closed his eyes, said a prayer, then bit into the ham and butter sandwich that sat before him. "Is there anything I can do to help this afternoon, *Daed*?"

Jacob did not look up from his meal. He did not like it when his son spoke with his mouth full. "*Nee*, Andy. Nothing needs doing."

It was obvious that Jacob was fibbing, but confronting his son would only cause Andy to lose face. Andy took another bite. Six months ago, he'd been his father's right hand on the farm, but his poor eyesight had rendered him a liability.

Chapter Four: Harvest Time

During the months following Albrecht's death, Andy's thoughts often drifted to the Yoder family and to the young widow. He replayed their meeting under the silver maple tree in his mind whenever he heard the cooing of the mourning dove. Her profound sadness clung to him like barnacles. Andy had encountered Lucy but once since that day. One afternoon, Andy came in from the farm and heard voices in the kitchen. His mother was entertaining Eleanor Yoder.

"How are you coping with this difficult situation?" Sarah Peachey had asked.

Eleanor had sighed. "As well as to be expected, I suppose."

"And how is Lucy? I thought she might come with you today?"

"She is well," Eleanor had said. "She wanted to come, but she felt unwell this morning."

Andy had frowned because Eleanor's response seemed guarded. Unfortunately, his mother could not be counted upon to pry further. The question on the forefront of everyone's mind was whether Lucy would return to her own community. Unwilling to interfere, no one asked, and all wondered.

October arrived, and with it, the long days of the harvest. The Amish reaped what they had sown. Andy loved harvest time

—its smell, the freshly harvested crops, the autumn stews and winter vegetables. He could spy birds perched and waiting for grasshoppers and weevils to emerge before swooping down to scoop them up. His first harvest had been at five years old. His grandfather had surprised him in the morning with a brand-new straw hat.

"Every farmer needs a *gut* hat to keep the sun off his face."

The hat had been much too big for Andy, yet he had worn it daily. Eventually, he grew into it. There is nothing as precious as a gift used to make memories with beloved relatives. Ever since then, the harvest had been Andy's favorite time of year.

"Andy," Jacob Peachey said as he put down his spoon and looked across the breakfast table.

Andy looked up at his father. It was a big day for them, as that day, they'd begin harvesting their largest crop of corn.

"After breakfast, I need you to take the buggy into town and fetch the new spring for the reaper."

Andy frowned. He'd been expecting his father to assign him a chore in the fields, not a menial task. During the previous year's harvest, Andy had steered six draft horses while towing the hammer mill. "Are you sure, *Daed*? I thought you would need help with the harvest."

"We have plenty of hands," Jacob reassured his son. "You'd be more help to me going into town and getting that spring."

Andy nodded. He spooned a mouthful of porridge into his mouth. His mind was working furiously. He had to convince his folks that his eyesight was not as bad as it seemed. His first strategy, hiding it, had backfired, for he'd become clumsy. While mucking the horse stall, he'd dropped the rake in the shavings. Reaching for where he thought it'd fallen had got him a handful of manure. He'd sidestepped it, only to tread on the rake, whose handle had hit him in the nose, sending him reeling backwards into the wheelbarrow. His father had caught the tail end of the debacle when Andy had been sitting in the wagon, feet in the air, his turdy hands unable to get a grip to lift himself up. Hence, his father had revoked Andy's responsibilities on the farm.

"I'll see you all later," Jacob said, rising from his chair. He leaned over and kissed Sarah on the forehead.

"Be careful," Sarah said.

Sarah worried during the harvest time. Some hands were new, the horses were skittish, and there were much heavier machines for the animals to haul. Furthermore, the bales and bushels were heavy.

"We always are," Jacob promised.

"I'll bring you all some lunch a little later," Sarah promised.

"Maybe Andy can help you," Jacob suggested. "He should be back from town by then."

Andy said nothing. His frustration mounted. Making lunch during the harvest was women's work. How could his old man push him aside?

Jacob turned to Andy. "Take Buddy," he instructed. "And be careful on the roads with him. The rains we had a few weeks back caused some damage. Parts of the road have eroded."

Andy nodded and watched his father go.

"Your *daed* is not trying to be unkind," Sarah said. "He is just trying to protect you."

Andy nodded, but it did not make the situation any easier. He was the only son. The farm was his legacy. Unable to be a farmer was something he needed to mourn. The bargaining stage was where Andy had pitched his tent, convinced that he'd find a way to see and continue the family legacy. Anger and sadness soon followed once he realized that his future was gone.

"You'd better get going," Sarah said.

Andy nodded and got up from the table. He picked up his straw hat before leaving. Andy walked a short distance from the back door to the barn. All the horses were being used for the harvest, save for old Buddy, his grandfather's old horse. He was long past his prime, yet he was still strong enough to pull the buggy.

"Come on old boy," Andy murmured as he led the horse outside of the barn. He harnessed the horse to the buggy and then set off. His father had been right: the late rains had wreaked havoc on the old dirt road. Potholes and crevices pockmarked the road. Andy was careful to steer Buddy around the dangerous parts. They passed the Yoder house. A figure stood in the window, then quickly retreated into the shadows.

Before long, Andy arrived in town.

"*Gude mariye*, Mr. Hershberger," he said as he stepped into the farm supply store.

"Andy!" the older man replied. "It's *gut* to see you." Mr. Hershberger had been working at the farm supply store for as long as Andy could remember. "You've come to pick up the spring?"

Andy nodded. Mr. Hershberger disappeared, then re-emerged with the new spring. "There you go," he said.

"*Danki*," Andy replied.

The door opened, and a crowd of farmers came into the store.

"Busy time of year," Andy remarked.

"Harvest season," Mr. Hershberger said. "Always something to repair."

Andy thanked the man before leaving the store. A familiar

figure approached him from a distance. It was not her shape but the effect she had on his heart that revealed to Andy who it was: Lucy Yoder. His heart skipped. Andy had not seen her since the funeral. She was dressed in black and walked with her mother-in-law. Andy climbed onto the buggy and made his way down the road in the direction of the Yoder women. He hoped to offer them a ride back to their farm. However, the women entered a shop and disappeared. Andy continued his journey, alone. This latest distraction took his attention off the road. Andy heard a loud crack followed by a piercing whinny. Buddy collapsed. Andy jumped from the buggy, but he knew without looking that the horse had broken its leg.

"I'm so sorry, boy," Andy whispered to the horse. He ran home. Jacob saw him running through the gate. He feared the worst.

"What happened?" Jacob asked.

Andy shook his head. He was panting. His face was stained with tears. "It's Buddy," he choked.

"Where is he?" Jacob asked. "What happened?"

"I don't know," Andy admitted. "He fell, and his leg is broken."

Jacob's face paled. He was not an emotional man, but Buddy was the last piece of his father on the farm. With Buddy gone, the old man's presence would die with him.

Andy waited for his father to say something, but he did not. Instead, Jacob turned around and walked toward the house. He emerged with his shotgun. Jacob walked right past Andy and in the direction of the main road. The back door slammed and foot-steps approached.

"What's happened?"

"It's Buddy. He's broken his leg."

"Oh no."

Andy turned to his mother and shook his head. "It was an accident," he whispered.

"It will be all right," she replied.

Andy wanted to believe her, but in that moment, it felt as if nothing would be all right ever again. A gunshot echoed.

Chapter Five: The Painter's Box

No one mentioned the incident with Buddy again. Nevertheless, it lingered. The dead horse reincarnated into the elephant in the room. Andy's mistake had pushed father and son further apart. By November, the Peachey house echoed of things left unsaid.

Andy was seldom asked to help anymore, not even by his long-suffering mother. Although his failure to protect Buddy had been a lapse in concentration, his father no longer trusted him with responsibilities due to his eyesight. In fact, he blamed him for being blind.

One afternoon, in the middle of November, Andy was home alone. His parents had gone into town together to visit some friends. Andy had been invited but had declined. Jacob had seemed relieved. It did not bother him that his only son was a recluse.

"You might do some washing," Sarah had suggested before leaving.

Andy had nodded. He was growing so used to helping his mother out with house chores that it hardly stung his manliness anymore. At least he had one parent's attention now that his father was disinclined to seek his help on the farm.

Shortly after his parents left the house, Andy headed down

to the basement to fetch the washing basins. The basement was used for washing and for the community church when it was the Peacheys' turn to host. It was nice to have church there in the heat of the summer. His basement was the coolest place to be.

As Andy stepped into the dimly lit basement, he shivered. Pale light was pouring in through the narrow window on the west side, and in the cold light, he could dimly make out the lay of the room. The basement was sparsely decorated with a table and a few chairs against the south-facing wall. There was a large cupboard in the corner where Sarah Peachey stored canned food and dry supplies such as flour and sugar. On the eastern wall was a long, solid wood countertop which held the two basins, one for washing and the other for rinsing. His mother had left a basket of dirty laundry beside them. Beneath them were storage cupboards.

Andy walked over to the basins and filled them with water. From a small, ceramic soap dish, he took the laundry soap and scrubbed the laundry. It was soap he'd helped his mother make. He found comfort in its clean, caustic smell. After he had finished, Andy missed the dish when replacing the soap, which slipped off the basin and onto the floor under the cupboards. Andy sighed. His eyesight was now a liability in the house, too. He knelt to retrieve the soap, using his fingers to feel any trail of slime rather than his eyes to spot it. His hands came upon something. It a wooden box with a lid. Andy had never seen the box before, nor had anyone touched it given the layer of dust on the lid. Andy wiped the top of the box using his sleeve, then got up from the floor, forgetting the soap under the counter.

Andy placed the mysterious box away on the table, far from the basin so as not to risk getting it wet. He ran his hands up and down the box until he felt a small hook latch. He unfastened it and opened the lid. The box had seven compartments. One large central compartment was flanked by two smaller compartments on each side. One narrow compartment ran along the bottom of the box, while three small square ones crowned the arrangement. The central compartment held an assortment of white tubes with small black caps. He picked one up to examine it. It was a tube of paint. The side compartments stored small sponges, an eraser, some tape, and a small jar of brush cleaner. In the longest compartment was a collection of paintbrushes, varying in thickness and length. Andy carefully examined every item before replacing them in the exact spot. He had never seen a painter's box before, and he wondered from where it came. A small drawer was at the base of the box. Andy pulled it open to reveal a stack of cream cards. He pulled them out and saw that they were all blank, save for one which read: *For Eli—Every blank card is a new journey.*

Andy frowned. Eli was his grandfather. He could not remember a time that his grandfather painted. Painting was not something the *Ordung* permitted except for practical purposes. Artistic pursuits were disallowed unless the art had a practical function.

Andy looked inside the painter's box again, and he saw that nothing had been used. Everything was brand new. His grandfather could never have been a painter. Time stood still as Andy pondered the mystery.

"Andy?" his mother called. "Are you here?"

Andy slammed the lid of the box. He heard the footsteps above him. Acting quickly, he returned the box to its hiding place and headed back upstairs.

For the next several days, Andy tried to solve the mystery of Eli's box. His imagination ran wild with theories, but they made no sense. He was desperate to inspect it again to search for other clues, but the opportunity eluded him.

Then, one day after lunch, he was given the chance that he's been waiting for.

"Mrs. Hershberger is sick," Sarah announced. "So, your *daed* is going to take me into town to see her."

"Will she be all right?" Andy asked.

Sarah nodded. "*Ya*, it's just a head cold. I will take her some soup, and hopefully, she'll feel better soon."

Jacob and Sarah left, so Andy bolted downstairs to retrieve the painter's box from under the cupboard. Andy carried it over to the table and sat down. He unlatched the box and removed a paintbrush and a tube of white paint. He placed them on the table and pulled the small drawer out to remove a blank cream-colored card. The adrenaline rush of doing something forbidden dizzied the frosted Amish boy. He opened the tube of paint and pressed a dollop of paint onto the brush like squeezing tooth-paste onto a toothbrush. And it was thus, with the familiarity of dental hygiene, that Andy's foray into the forbidden began.

Andy took a deep breath as he positioned the paintbrush. His hand trembled as he hovered above the card. He inhaled, steadied himself, and began to paint. As he painted, Andy was amazed to see a small, red-breasted nuthatch form before his very eyes. The fact that his hand could, through a brush, transfer an image from his mind onto paper exhilarated him.

Andy found any excuse to sneak off to paint whenever the opportunity presented itself. He felt no guilt despite imagining his parents' disapproval. Instead, he relished this newfound satisfaction that he had something to contribute to the world. It was good to feel normal again. He could forget all that he'd lost, cease to mourn all that had been taken from him, and finally find something he could control and in which he could accomplish something successfully.

Each day, Andy painted birds. By doing so, he learned something new about himself. He was not just a poor farm boy steadily losing his sight. He was an artist who possessed a natural, creative instinct that allowed him to create. He was talented! Granted, it had to be kept a secret. Andy hid his paintings in the drawer of the painter's box beneath the note written for his grandfather.

One morning, Andy found his mother standing in the living room. She was holding something in her hand. Andy could not see.

"What is that?" Andy asked.

"A *Grischtdaag* card from our cousins in Pennsylvania," Sarah explained.

"Isn't it a bit early?"

"You know what they are like; as soon as November arrives, they are ready to celebrate *Grischtdaag*." Sarah propped the card up on the mantelpiece. "I love getting *Grischtdaag* cards. They are small things that offer much joy."

Andy waited for his mother to leave the room. Once she was in the kitchen, he stepped toward the mantelpiece to study the card. The winter scene on the front of the card struck the boy with an idea.

∞∞∞

Andy painted a tree on the card before him, ensuring perfection in every detail. He was consumed in his work such that he did not hear a young boy calling him from outside. When a pebble struck the narrow basement window, Andy was startled.

"Noah!" Andy said, walking over to the window and opening it. "What are you doing?"

Noah's face was flushed. He was unable to speak.

"Wait there," Andy instructed. A moment later, he was standing out in the yard with Noah. The young boy had managed to catch his breath. "She caught me," Noah explained.

"Who?"

"Lucy Yoder," Noah explained.

"How?"

Noah shrugged. "She was just waiting for me, and when I put the envelope down, she opened the door and chased after me."

"But she doesn't know who you are," Andy reasoned.

Noah grimaced.

"What?" Andy asked.

"Mr. Yoder saw me too."

Andy's face paled when he realized that Lucy Yoder now knew. He thought of the unfinished fir tree sitting on his desk that would never be sent.

Chapter Six: The Things Left Unsaid

Outside, a blizzard had raged for hours, dumping three feet of snow and keeping the Peacheys cooped up for two days. Andy had been desperate to return outdoors. Once the storm had cleared, he dressed warmly and headed outside. The air was icy, and the sky was pale. Andy stood on the edge of his family's property, gazing at the horizon. He could hear birds again. Frustrated that he could not see clearly to the hills, woods, and neighbors, Andy closed his eyes, inhaled, and reconciled himself to Christmas' galloping approach: a mere ten days until December twenty-fifth. Family from Pennsylvania would soon be visiting, and the house would be bustling with relatives.

As Andy opened his eyes, a silhouette approached. His heart skipped a beat, then his stomach sank.

"Lucy," Andy said.

"Was it you?" Lucy demanded. "Answer me."

Unable to make eye contact for the fury in Lucy's eyes, Andy hung his head. "It was me," he admitted. His concession calmed the girl. Her shoulders relaxed, and she leaned back on her heels. Then, like lightning on dry brush, anger danced in her eyes.

"How could you do something so cruel?" Lucy accused.

Andy was taken aback. He was ashamed at having been caught, but never had he wanted to torture the widow. Besides, who sends Christmas cards as an act of cruelty? "I don't understand."

Tears spewed down Lucy's face. "The initial—the "A." I thought that they were from Albrecht."

Andy felt faint. His simple signature had been used to keep his art a secret. It had never dawned on him that it could have been confused—and to such magnitude. He cursed himself for his monumental oversight.

Lucy had turned her back to Andy to stare at the hills in the distance. Her arms were wrapped around her body, more for comfort than for warmth. Indeed, she trembled beneath her shawl.

Recognizing the need to explain his gifts, Andy finally spoke up. "Please know that I did not send you those cards because I wished to hurt you."

"Then, why? Didn't you and Albrecht stop speaking to each other? Wasn't this your way of continuing your feud?" Lucy turned to look at Andy. The wind had picked up, flailing strands of her hair about her face, compounding her inner turmoil with flagellation. Tears froze to her cheeks. Nevertheless, her gaze was unwavering, unnerving the man. Words fled him. Thus, he could not formulate a good explanation. He held his tongue so as not to come up with a bad one.

She looks fragile, Andy thought, for hers was a pain even the blind could see. "I wish that I could explain, but I can't."

Lucy frowned. Through gritted teeth, she retorted, "You can't? Or you won't?"

Andy shook his head. "I am sorry for any pain that I've

caused."

Lucy huffed. "I shouldn't have come. This was a mistake." She turned and ran before Andy could manage another word.

"Lucy! Wait!" Andy's words were carried into the wind and never delivered to Lucy.

Teeth chattering, he returned home, dejected.

"Andy? Is everything all right?" Sarah Peachey asked. "You've hardly touched your food. Are you unwell?"

Andy did not make eye contact with his mother, choosing, instead, to stare into his plate of untouched supper. His stomach turned. His encounter with Lucy weighed heavily on his mind. Lucy's despair and disappointment haunted him. He replayed their conversation, re-imagined it, and changed what he said, hoping for a different reaction, but it all was the same. He could not explain himself. It had been a feeling that had prompted him to do it. His guilt ate away at his appetite.

"What was the young Yoder girl doing here this afternoon?" Jacob asked.

Andy had not known that anyone else had seen her.

"Lucy was here?" Sarah asked with interest. "What did she want?"

Andy was still at a loss for words. The English language simply abandoned him on the day. Fortunately for him, there was a knock at the door.

"That will be Noah," Jacob said. "I told him to come and find me when he was done mucking out the animal stalls so I could inspect his work."

Jacob rose from the table and left the room.

"May I also be excused?" Andy asked.

"Are you sure you won't eat?"

Andy shook his head. His mother sighed. A mother knows that a loss of appetite in a man can only mean sickness, be it the heart or body.

"I will cover it for you in case you are hungry later."

Andy nodded his gratitude and rose. "I'm going to take a walk."

"At this hour?" Sarah asked.

"I won't be long."

Andy had no plan for where to go. He let his feet carry him, choosing to be entranced by his thoughts. They led him straight to the Yoder front porch. When he snapped out of his trance, he felt the urge to run, yet his feet were now locked into place. As though their betrayal weren't enough, words lit up his morosity, some brighter than others, pointing the way to true north. He had his explanation for Lucy. It was time to make things right.

Andy cleared his throat and knocked. Footsteps approached; the curtain was pulled aside to reveal Moses Yoder. The man's eyes were colder than winter's wind. Andy shivered. Lucy and Eleanor Yoder stood behind him in the hallway, a mirror image of when Andy had met Lucy for the first time.

"Mr. Yoder," Andy said. "I am sorry to interrupt you during dinner time, but may I speak with Lucy?"

Moses frowned. "Don't you think that you've done enough."

"*Nee*, sir. I've not made things right. She left before I had the chance to explain. I am here to do just that."

Moses stared at Andy, processing the young man's words. With a grunt and a stiff nod, Moses closed the curtain. "Wait here," he instructed.

There were words spoken in hushed tones, followed by silence, then footsteps away from the door. Andy wondered if they'd all simply gone back to their dinner. The door opened, and there stood Lucy wearing her shawl. She wrapped it tightly around herself and stepped out.

Andy exhaled. "I am sorry about this afternoon," he began.

"Do you have an explanation?" Lucy was impatient.

Andy did not blame her. It was chilly. She likely wished to return indoors. "Yes."

Lucy said nothing. The sun had just disappeared. The trees stretched their branches into the twilight as though reaching up to pull down the moon. Their shadows made it impossible for Andy to read Lucy's face, not with his failing sight.

Andy sighed. "On the day of Albrecht's funeral, I found you standing under the silver maple tree. You asked me about the mourning dove." He paused. He had hoped to gauge whether Lucy remembered the day, but dusk overshadowed her.

Lucy frowned. She had no recollection. She waited for him to continue.

"I walked home that afternoon empathizing with you. I recognized a part of me inside of you."

"I don't understand," Lucy said quietly.

"I saw your loss and your pain. I recognized it because I, too, have those feelings. I know what it feels like to fall apart, especially when you are trying hard to hold yourself together."

A candle was lit in the front room window. It shone across Lucy's face. Her eyes were soft, and something glistened on her cheeks.

"I lost a great childhood friend. Albrecht and I never had a falling out, just a growing apart. To see his widow shattered me. I could see when his brothers died. He looked like he was mourning not only who they were but also who they would become.

He would never know what they would be like as husbands and fathers. He cried because he would never get to meet his sisters-in-law."

Lucy sniffled to mute her cry.

"Once you arrived, we figured that there was a future for Albrecht that he had wanted for his siblings. Then, seeing you mourn, and hearing the dove cry, I was moved to do something." Andy cleared his throat, hoping to send the lump in it back down. "I found my grandfather's old painting kit. It had been given to my *groossdaadi*, but he never used it. I just picked up a paintbrush, and it came to me as easily as breathing. I loved it. Life had taken much away from me, but it had hidden this away in our basement. When my *maem* received a *Grischtdaag* card from our family in Pennsylvania, it made her happy. I thought of you and how crushed you had seemed on the day of the funeral. It gave me an idea."

"To make me a *Grischtdaag* card?" Lucy asked.

Andy nodded. "I thought it might make you smile. I had seen what losing his brothers had done to Albrecht. To then see it on his widow's face—" Andy sniffed, then exhaled.

"If you only intended to send the one card, why so many more?"

Andy cleared his throat. "To see if it had worked."

"What do you mean?"

"I had asked Noah to hide after he had delivered the first card to see your reaction when you opened it. I was curious to know if you liked it. He told me that you'd taken it inside. So I sent a second card."

"Which I opened on the porch. Was Noah watching?"

Andy nodded. "He said that when you opened the envelope,

your face changed. He described it as the sun pushing through clouds. You were beaming, he said. So, I couldn't stop. Not when they had that effect on you."

"*Danki* for coming here tonight and telling me this." Lucy paused as though about to continue.

Andy waited for her to say something else, but she didn't. The front door opened, then shut. Only then did Andy realize that he stood alone on the porch.

Chapter Seven: The Red-Breasted Nuthatch

A ndy sat in his rocking chair staring out onto the snow-swept landscape. The blizzard had left over ten inches of snow, and while the sun had shone over the last few days, the temperature remained so low that the snow had crusted. A figure appeared at the garden gate. He removed the small blanket from his lap and got up from his chair. He walked over to the window to get a better look. The figure approached, pulled open the gate, and walked up the snowy path toward the house. Once onto the porch, Andy gasped. It was Lucy Yoder!

"I hope you do not mind that I came," she said upon taking the final step.

Andy shook his head.

His mother inquired as to who it was. "I thought that I heard a woman's voice. What a nice surprise!"

Lucy smiled. "I am sorry to come by unannounced. I just walked past and thought that I would stop in because I know I never thanked you properly for the basket you sent after—" Her voice trailed, leaving the sentence hanging in the air.

"Have a cup of tea?" Sarah asked.

Lucy hesitated. Andy thought she might decline the invitation, but to his surprise, she nodded. "That would be nice."

"Why don't you two go and sit by the fire in the living room?" Sarah suggested. "I'll fetch the tea."

"Do you need any help?" Lucy offered.

"*Nee, danki*," Sarah declined. "You just go and get warm."

Andy led the way into the living room. "You take the seat by the fire."

Lucy smiled before moving to the soft chair near the mantel. She sat down and looked around the room. Her hands were clasped in her lap. Andy wondered if she was nervous or perhaps, uncomfortable.

"I'm sorry," Lucy volunteered.

"What for?" Andy asked.

"My being here is not by chance," she whispered. "I came with a purpose, but when your *maem* appeared, I couldn't think of what to say."

Andy nodded. He was grateful that Lucy had not revealed the true reason for her visit. Indeed, his parents were unaware of his Christmas cards. Surely they would not approve of the art he made in their basement.

"Why did you come?" Andy whispered.

"I've been thinking about what you said the other day when you came to the house. I wanted to tell you that despite everything, those cards you sent did help me."

"Really?" Andy asked. He was incredulous as to her turnaround.

Lucy nodded. "At first it was hard to separate the cards from Albrecht because I needed to believe it. However, after you left, I looked at the cards again. They still brought me comfort despite knowing they were from you.

Andy looked at Lucy with a mixture of relief and gratitude. Because his mind could not decide which to feel, his face looked confused, making it difficult for Lucy to read how he felt. Finally, relief that the cards had served their purpose won out, and he relaxed. Lucy's smile made Andy feel warmer than the fire did.

Sarah entered the room carrying a tray. "Here we go."

Andy jumped up, took the tray from her, and set it down on the table.

"So, what have you two been talking about?" Sarah asked, sitting down next to Andy.

"Just the weather," Lucy lied.

Sarah nodded, unsuspecting. She handed Lucy her cup. "Here you go."

"*Danki*," Lucy said. "It's nice to be in from the cold."

"It's a pleasure to have you here. Tell me, how are your in-laws?"

"They are well, all things considered." Her words hung in the air. Lucy took another sip of her tea.

"Will you be going home to your folks for *Grischtdaag*?" Sarah asked.

Shyly, Lucy shook her head.

"Won't they miss you?" Sarah pried.

"Perhaps, but—" Lucy paused to choose her words—"I don't want the Yoders to be alone."

Oh, Sarah mouthed. She sipped her tea.

"How are you?" Andy ventured. "This must be difficult for you, too."

Lucy nodded. "It is, but I've some small comforts." She eyed Andy. "*Danki* for asking." Lucy finished her tea, set her cup down, and got up. "I should get going. *Danki* again, Mrs. Peachey, for the basket."

"*Gaern gschehne*. Please, come again soon," Sarah said warmly.

Andy escorted the young lady to the front door. He opened the door. Lucy stepped out and motioned for him to do the same. Andy complied though he was not dressed for the occasion.

"I still have some questions about the cards," Lucy confessed.

Andy nodded.

"May I come back tomorrow?"

Andy was not so sure. He had much to lose should his parents overhear their conversation. He had to think quickly. Andy looked into her eyes, for men always find inspiration in the beauty of a young woman. "If the weather is clear, I will go birding tomorrow. You can come along if you would like." *You genius!* he told himself. *Way to turn this into a date!*

Lucy nodded. "I will come after breakfast."

"See you tomorrow, then," Andy said.

Lucy walked down the porch steps and back along the path to the front gate. Andy gazed at her. His teeth chattered, but he did not budge. Only when she had disappeared from view did he venture back into the house. After making sure his mother wasn't around, he couldn't help but click his heels.

The next morning, Andy stood awaiting Lucy on his porch. He had packed a light snack and his binoculars—though not for him. He figured Lucy could use them. When she approached, he hurried to meet her, taking the steps two at a time, binoculars bouncing jauntily against his chest.

"I thought we might take a walk to the lake," Andy said, skipping the usual greeting formalities.

It was as though a shadow passed over Lucy's face. Andy looked up to see if there were any clouds in the sky. It was clear and blue.

"Unless you prefer to go somewhere else?"

"*Nee*," Lucy fibbed. "The lake is fine."

Andy smiled, nerves buzzing. He could not remember ever feeling this way. "Let's go, then."

The pair walked along the main road toward the lake. Forgetting the reason for her visit, Andy chatted her up, thinking only about the birds (and the bees).

"Have you been birding before?" Andy asked.

Lucy shook her head. "I grew up in town since my *daed* is a shopkeeper, and none of the Yoders are birders."

Andy nodded. "My *groossdaadi* was a birder. He used to take me out when I was a child. It's been a great love of mine ever since."

Lucy frowned.

"What is it?"

"Nothing," Lucy said, shaking her head.

"You can tell me," Andy assured her.

Lucy stopped walking.

"I hope it's not rude," she said. "Or that I am not overstepping, but Mrs. Yoder told me about your...condition."

Andy nodded. He waited for her to continue.

"So, I was just wondering, how you manage to still go birding."

"My eyesight's only deteriorated since Albrecht"—Andy stopped himself —"in the last few months. Now, I hear them. When I do, I can imagine them. That's how I see them again. Just like the trees and the lake. That's how I can paint them."

"It must be hard." Lucy feigned empathy, not wanting Andy to think she didn't care about his plight, but in reality, she only wanted to keep Andy talking to see if he would reveal anything about her beloved Albrecht.

"Some days are harder than others," Andy admitted.

"I can relate," Lucy offered. "What about the binoculars?"

"Oh! Occasionally I use them, but they're for you." Andy blushed.

They continued to walk under the cloudless sky. The air was crisp, and there was no breeze. Upon arriving at the lake's edge, Lucy had her breath taken away.

"It's just like the first card," Lucy whispered.

Andy nodded. "When we were kids, Albrecht and I used to come skating here all the time. This is one of my favorite places to come in the winter. The ice is not yet thick enough for skating, but come January, all you'll hear are peals of laughter harmonized to the scraping of the skates sliding across the ice. It's magical."

Lucy's eyes burned. She blinked back tears. "Albrecht promised we'd come and skate." She closed her eyes to see what might have been.

"I hear something," Andy said. He closed his eyes.

Lucy opened her eyes. She heard a series of soft whistles and warbles. "What is it?"

"I think it's a Dark-eyed Junco," Andy said. He made his way toward the call, careful to stay out of the water. He was cautious with his footing yet eager to show off his find. He slipped, fell, then bounced back up. Lucy followed, unable to help him. Andy stopped. He lifted his binoculars to his eyes. "There it is," he whispered.

Lucy saw a small bird perched on a branch high above them. Andy handed her the binoculars. The bird's plumage matched its surroundings. The dark brown of its back blended in with the bark of the tree, while its white underbelly matched the snow beneath the tree.

"She's beautiful," Lucy said.

"She is," Andy agreed.

An hour circling the lake went by in a flash. Andy identified the birds for Lucy and gave her mnemonics to help her remember each species. He had her close her eyes and describe each of their calls. The young woman had never been so engrossed by nature before. The warmth of their burgeoning friendship kept away the nip in the air. The winter sun cheered the pair. For sixty minutes, they'd forgotten their grief.

"I did not know that birds could be so interesting," Lucy said. "*Danki* for inviting me."

"*Gaern gschehne,*" Andy replied. "It's a joy for me to be able to share something I love with another who'll appreciate it. Birding with my *groossdaadi* gave me some of my most cherished memories."

Lucy smiled. Andy squinted at its brightness. *Could it be her first truly happy smile since Albrecht?* he wondered. Her smile suddenly faded.

"What is the time?" Lucy asked. "I promised Eleanor I would be home to help with lunch."

Andy looked up at the sun. "It's not quite midday." He looked to her. "If we leave now, we should be back in time."

They packed up to walk back around the lake toward the road. "This will be the quickest way home for you," Andy said. Then, it dawned on him: they had only spoken of fowl. "I fear that I may have distracted you with the birds. What was it you wanted to ask me?"

Lucy nodded, looking pensive. "When Eleanor discovered the cards and I told her that I thought they were from Albrecht, she explained that your community's *Ordnung* does not allow for its members to practice artistic pursuits. Is your talent a secret?"

Andy nodded.

"But does painting not make you feel guilty? For surely if the *Ordnung* says you should not paint, it is because *Gott* does not wish it."

"The *Ordnung* of our *gmay* does ban the practice of artistic pursuits. They are perceived as wasteful and vain unless they have a purpose. When painting those cards for you, I had a purpose: I was giving comfort."

Lucy squinted, trying to rectify the situation in her head.

"When I started painting, it was out of curiosity. Now, though, when I look across a blank page, it feels as though the whole world is open before me. For years, my world has been shrinking, darkening. When I paint, it's as if the world is growing again. Painting expands my horizons, when, without it, I can't see the horizon."

Lucy stood still.

"The first bird my *groossdaadi* ever pointed out to me was a Red-breasted Nuthatch. I can still remember it. I could probably paint it for you—the memory is so vivid. It was in the middle of summer, and it took me ages to find the bird among the thick bushes. My *groossdaadi* was pointing to it, describing it, even trying to look through the binoculars with me to quicken the endeavor. When I finally did—I can remember the flutter of excitement and the smile on my *groossdaadi's* face." Andy paused and bowed his head in reverence for his grandfather. "The years before my *groossdaadi* died, I watched his eyesight fade. I became his eyes. We would go out together to look for birds. While he could no longer see them, he listened to their songs. I am terrified of the day when I'll hear the song of the Red-breasted Nuthatch but where I won't be able to look up and see it. When I paint, the pain of losing my vision eases and the bird is brought down from a high branch in a tall tree to lay before me."

Lucy nodded, deep in thought. "Mmm, I see." Her pun escaped her.

"We will soon be back home," Andy said. "Do you have anything else you wanted to ask me?"

"I was wondering about the themes and the words for the *Grischtdaag* cards? How did you choose them? How did you know what would speak to me?"

Andy shrugged. "I didn't. I first started by painting birds. Then I decided to paint simple themes about life in our *gmay*. I chose what spoke to me. I suppose they meant something to you, too, since we're both grieving."

Lucy's eyebrows furrowed. The Yoder homestead galloped toward them. Unwilling to miss an opportunity, Andy asked, "Can we do this again?"

Lucy hesitated.

"It's been nice to have someone to talk to," Andy admitted, "someone whose world has changed as much as mine in the last few months."

"It has," Lucy agreed.

"Might we take another walk tomorrow, then?" Andy asked.

Again, Lucy hesitated. She had enjoyed their walk. Andy Peachey had been friendly and kind. It was good to be with someone her own age. Also, there was still so much she wanted to know about Albrecht as a child. That was the clincher. "*Ya*. We can walk again tomorrow."

"I will come by your house in the morning," Andy promised with a smile beaming brighter than the sun.

Chapter Eight: Lost Star

"I'm not sure that it's a *gut* idea," Eleanor said. Her spoon hovered in midair above her half-eaten bowl of porridge, afraid to finish its journey to her face due to the frown it wore. "I don't want you to get hurt again."

"It's just a walk," Lucy protested.

Eleanor placed her spoon down in the bowl and sighed. Every morning for the past week, Andy Peachey had been standing at the bottom of the garden waiting for Lucy to finish her chores. The minute the chores were complete, the two went off on long walks together. It was not the fact that Lucy had a new friend that bothered Eleanor; it was her concern that Lucy might become attached to Andy. It seemed imprudent.

"I am not going to get hurt," Lucy assured her mother-in-law. "All Andy wants to do is walk and talk about Albrecht and look at birds. It's completely harmless."

Eleanor frowned. She looked to her husband across the table. Moses was determined not to get involved. He kept his eyes on his breakfast and ate it quickly.

Seeing no ally in her spouse yet certain of her protective instincts, Eleanor continued her inquisition. "And have you asked him about his condition?" Eleanor asked Lucy. "Does he discuss it with you?"

It was known that Andy had poor eyesight, yet few outside of the family knew the details.

"It's deteriorating," Lucy deadpanned. She held her cards close to her chest in an effort to protect her new friend. Andy had said that his condition was changing his life for the worse. The comfort the cards brought to him and to her was still a secret. Lucy had given her in-laws a watered-down version of the Christmas cards' origins. She had told them that Andy had felt bad about how he and Albrecht had grown apart, that he mourned with his widow, and that he had sent the cards as a gesture of good will. Lucy let on that Andy had purchased the cards from an English store. It would have been cruel to throw Andy under the buggy for his newfound artistic ways.

"Will he eventually go blind?" Eleanor asked.

Lucy shrugged. "I'd better get going." She got up from the table, cleared the dishes, and dressed for the outdoors. All the while, she could feel Eleanor's eyes piercing into her soul. The old woman had a read on her, but Lucy would do things her way. She could use Andy to discover more about Albrecht's past, a past unknown to his parents. A bit of birdwatching wouldn't hurt anybody.

"I am going now," Lucy announced.

Eleanor nodded but said nothing.

"*Sehn dich schpeeder* (See you later)," Moses said, sipping his coffee. He'd slowed his ingestion considerably since Eleanor and Lucy's conversation had ended.

Lucy walked into the hallway, put on her bonnet and shawl, then opened the door. A gust of wind blew in as a reminder to grab her mittens. As Lucy made her way back to her room, her in-laws began to speak.

"Do you really need to interrogate her?" Moses asked. "We've known Andy Peachey his whole life. He's gentle and respectful."

"It's not that I don't like Andy," Eleanor replied. "I don't think he and Lucy should be spending so much time together."

Moses sighed. A chair scraped the wooden floor. Lucy hurried out of the front door. Andy awaited her outside, and she hurried down the narrow path toward him.

"*Gude daag*," Andy said, smiling. He held open the small gate.

"*Gude daag*," Lucy replied. "*Wie geht's* (How's it going)?"

"*Gut*," Andy replied. "Although, I'm afraid that my *maem* caught me on the way out this morning and asked if we would walk into town. She needs a few things for the house. Do you mind?"

"That's fine," Lucy said.

Andy smiled. They turned to head toward the market. The skies were clear, but the nip whipped their behinds into a trot that they might keep warm. Andy cleared his throat. Lucy glanced sideways.

"So, my mother-in-law was worried about your eyesight. Does it keep you from using a buggy?"

Andy paused. Lucy stopped walking, too, though she worried she had struck a nerve. Andy sighed.

"I was fine until Buddy died," Andy volunteered. He looked to Lucy. She looked compassionate and curious. Andy decided to trust her. "Let's walk." As they did, he recounted the incident with his grandfather's horse, how it had caused a widening rift between him and his father, and how he had concluded that it was best for him to walk. Lucy's heart went out to him. Andy was not bitter or resentful about his failing eyesight. He was grieving a horse and his sight.

"Would you like to come to the school nativity play?" Andy's question was abrupt. The conversation had taken a quick turn.

Lucy looked surprised. Their community, just like her old one, held a nativity play every year. However, it was usually only attended by the families of the children.

"Noah will be in it," Andy explained as though reading her mind. "He's like family. He helps on the farm after school. He smiles all the time. He'll work for us on the weekends during harvest. His *groossmammi* has been sick and is too frail to attend. Noah was disappointed that no one would come to watch him, so I promised him that I would attend."

Lucy got the impression that Noah was like a younger brother. Indeed, the Peacheys had no other children. Perhaps watching the children's play would spark Christmas cheer in Lucy's heart.

"When is it?"

"Tomorrow evening," Andy replied.

"I think I will," Lucy said.

"Noah will be over the moon. He was hoping that you'd say you'd come."

"Well, then I'm happy to be there for him." Lucy looked up to see the roofs of the houses normally obscured by the leaves in the summer. In winter, homes were visible from the road. Thus, as they walked, Lucy noticed that people were watching them. Surely they were gossiping of the unusual friendship, finding fulfillment by discussing the latest scandal—or perceived one.

"I feel famous," Andy whispered. "Usually, I get the odd person glancing at me sympathetically, but when I'm with you, they all stare."

The embarrassment made Lucy's cheeks flush, yet she smiled. Her friend was happy, and, for once, she was not alone. A group of women spotted Andy and Lucy coming toward them. They stopped talking to gaze.

"*Gude mariye*," Andy said cheerfully.

Some murmurs of good morning came from the group.

"They always remind me of hens," Andy whispered as they approached the door, "the way that they all gather together ruffling their feathers and making indignant clucks at one another."

Lucy giggled. Then she laughed. Andy was right. The women did seem like they needed a rooster to keep them from pecking at each other and the passersby.

Once they made it to the store, Lucy said to Andy, "I'll wait out here for you."

"Are you sure?" Andy asked.

Lucy nodded.

"I won't be long," Andy promised as he headed into the store.

Lucy stood on the sidewalk and peered into the store window. There was a simple display of foodstuffs and haberdashery. Some of the items were on sale, while others, with the coming spring in mind, were new in stock. Lucy admired a light purple fabric and for the first time, felt uncomfortable in her stark black dress. While Lucy examined the items, a group of women spoke among themselves. They had not noticed that she had not gone into the store.

"Apparently, they go on long walks together. Mrs. King saw

them at the lake a few days ago, and then Mrs. Fisher saw them walking in the apple orchards."

"Well, I think it's nice that the poor girl has a friend after everything that she's been through."

"I agree. They seem to be *gut* for one another."

"I just worry that poor Andy will be heartbroken when she decides to go back home. Did you see the way he was looking at her just now?"

"Well, maybe she'll stay."

"Only if she plans on spending the rest of her life playing nurse to an ailing husband."

Lucy was so focused on trying to hear more of the ladies' conversation that she failed to notice that Andy was back by her side. "Shall we go?" Andy said, surprising his date.

Lucy jumped. "Please," Lucy begged.

They headed out of town, Andy not thinking of anything to talk about, Lucy preoccupied with the chatter she'd overheard. She had not thought that their friendship would be scrutinized so closely. And so soon! She enjoyed her time with Andy, but public perception made her shy, more so than she naturally was. *Should I cancel our plans to attend the nativity together?* she wondered.

"Have you ever been close to marriage?" Lucy blurted.

Taken aback, mouth agape, Andy shook his head.

Lucy nodded.

"It's not that I don't want to get married one day. It's just not that simple anymore." He glanced at her. "And you? Would you ever remarry?"

Lucy detected a note of interest in Andy's voice that made her feel as if he was asking her more than an innocent question, but before she had time to think of a reply, an oncoming buggy distracted them both.

"*Gude mariye,*" Andy called to the driver. He merely tipped his hat in response.

"Who was that?" Lucy asked.

"Mr. Livingston."

"Livingston?" Lucy said. "That doesn't sound Amish."

"You haven't heard of Mr. Livingston?" Andy asked, surprised. "He's an *Englisch* man who joined our *gmay* about forty years ago. It was quite the story back in the day."

"Mmm," Lucy murmured.

The two continued in silence since Andy didn't have the nerve to repeat his question and Lucy was too distracted to broach another subject. "So, I will see you tomorrow afternoon?" Andy asked as they reached the front gate of the Yoder farm.

Lucy frowned. She'd been preoccupied with the old hens.

"For the nativity play at the school?"

"*Ya,* of course," Lucy said.

"I will see you then," Andy said. He smiled and turned back to the road. Lucy made her way up the garden path. The front door's curtain swung closed. *Eleanor!* she thought. *Another hen.* Lucy shook her head. As she stepped onto the porch, Lucy turned to see Andy disappear around the bend. She was frustrated and concerned. Something was happening that was out of her control. A cock crowed, and hens clucked.

The following evening, Noah drove Andy in a buggy to the Yoders. Lucy had wrestled all day about whether to cancel. She was perturbed by the previous day's gossip. In the end, disappointing Noah was a price that she was unwilling to pay.

"*Gude daag,*" Lucy said as the buggy came to a stop.

"*Gude daag*," Andy said, smiling.

"Hello Mrs. Yoder," Noah said politely.

Lucy turned to look for her mother-in-law as she climbed up onto the buggy. Then it dawned on her that she was Mrs. Yoder. She was unaccustomed to the title. "Are you looking forward to the play?" Lucy asked, hoping to shake her despair.

"*Ya*," Noah exclaimed. "My teacher made me the donkey."

"That's *wunderbaar!*" Lucy said. "The donkey is a very important part of the story."

Noah beamed.

A beautifully carved nativity scene greeted all guests to the school. Andy explained that it was a community heirloom. Lucy gazed at the polished figurines. Mary and the Christ-child were especially poignant. Lucy swallowed the lump in her throat and moved to her seat. She and Andy felt it was only right to sit at the back to leave room for those with children nearer the front. When the children appeared, Noah smiled shyly. *It was right for us to come here,* Lucy thought.

Lucy was a veteran of acting in nativities. However, she was disconnected from this one. The children made all giggle. The parents shone their delight. Andy, who most certainly could not make them out from his seat, seemed tepidly engrossed, his head bobbing up when there was a donkey on set. Lucy, however, was crippled with pain. She struggled to breathe.

"I'm sorry, I need some air," Lucy whispered urgently to Andy. She arose to make her way out silently. Lucy gulped at the air in the schoolyard, yet it did not hold enough air for her. She cried for fear of suffocation. Her weeping lightened her chest, facilitating the airflow that now fueled her agony like a blower to hot coals. She blinked away the tears to prevent them from sealing her eyes shut. After all, she couldn't be as blind as Andy and expect to make it home safely.

Home! Where she had once shared a bed with Albrecht. Now he was gone, and any offspring he might have sired to comfort her had gone with him. Her grief tore at her chest to rip her heart out. She had held it in for too long and much too close to heart. It fought to get out.

Andy spied Lucy tugging her shawl tightly around her as if she were full of cracks, about to shatter into thousands of pieces. He made his way outside to offer some comfort.

"Are you all right?"

Lucy wept.

"What is it, Lucy?" Andy asked, stepping closer.

Lucy shook her head. "It's nothing," Lucy whispered.

Andy made his way to the short stone wall that marked off the schoolyard from the neighbors. "You know, Albrecht and I used to pretend that this wall was special, that on this side was the schoolyard, but if we stepped onto the other side, we could be anywhere in the world."

Lucy sniffled. "Where did you go?"

"I don't remember. I do remember that Albrecht was always a much better storyteller than I was."

"He did have a way with words." Lucy sat down beside Andy. Stars filled the sky, yet without Albrecht, the heavens were void. After a heavy, silent pause, she continued. "Nobody knew, except Albrecht. We thought it'd be wiser to keep it to ourselves until we were passed the first trimester. I was so excited. I'd dreamed of having *kinner* my whole life."

Lucy gazed up into the void, hoping to see a familiar face. Andy eyed her attentively.

"I don't know what happened," Lucy continued. "It was like the moment before dawn when the last star is visible in the sky and then it's gone."

"Did you see a doctor?"

Lucy shook her head. Then she felt something. She looked down from the sky and to her lap. Andy's hand was on hers.

"We should probably go back inside," Lucy said. "Noah will wonder where we've gone."

"Are you sure you're fine going back inside?" Andy asked.

Lucy nodded. She let the momentum of her rising take her hand from beneath his and returned to the schoolhouse ahead of Andy.

Noah found them both at the end of the show. Lucy hugged the boy. "That was *wunderbaar*."

Andy clapped him on the back. "Let's get you home so you can tell your *groossmammi* all about it."

Noah nodded.

"How about you drive us home and we'll sit in the buggy?" Andy suggested. Noah obliged, flattered by the independence and trust given to him. Andy, however, seized the opportunity to discuss things further with Lucy. Once they were settled and moving, Andy spoke up.

"What's on your mind?"

Lucy looked out of the window. There was nothing to see with darkness blanketing everything, but she felt secure this way—less vulnerable. Then, they passed the Fisher farm. "I was thinking of what my life might have been like had I made different decisions. What if I'd never agreed to go to the *sing* at the Fisher's farm; then I would never have met Albrecht and my life would have been entirely different."

"Is that what you wished had happened? How could you be sure it would have been desirable?"

Lucy was still. "It would have been better than the pain I feel now?"

"Are you sure?"

Lucy bristled. She was used to wallowing alone. This challenge to her self-pity was unwelcome. Feeling feisty, as she was no longer shy with Andy, she returned serve. "Are you suggesting that what I am enduring now is better than what could have been?"

"I am asking if you can be sure of what could have been better." Andy paused to let his words sink in. "How could you be sure that you wouldn't have met Albrecht elsewhere?"

"So, you believe that two people are destined to be together?"

"I am saying that the *sing* at the Fisher farm was only one of a myriad of ways you could have met Albrecht. If it was meant to be..." Andy paused. "*Gott* gave us the free will to make our own choices. Nevertheless, He has a hand in choosing whom we shall meet and where we shall go. Think of Jonah. He was going to go to Nineveh whether or not he got on the boat to Tarsus. Likewise, *Gott* knows the right people for us to marry and bring us joy. I believe that *Gott* would have prepared it so that you and Albrecht would have met and married no matter the choices you made."

Lucy narrowed her eyes. "Do you truly believe that I was destined to suffer this heartache and loss?"

Andy shook his head. "There is no happiness in life without loss and hurt. They walk together hand in hand. If you had never met Albrecht, you might not have become a young widow, but

113

you also would not have experienced the profound love and joy that he made you feel."

"Albrecht said something similar to me once," Lucy admitted. "He said that nothing lasts forever. That is why we need to feel every moment, both the happy parts and sad ones. 'It's part of being alive,' he said."

"He was right," Andy concurred.

It impressed Lucy that Andy sounded like Albrecht. If she closed her eyes and listened to him speak, it almost seemed as if Albrecht were speaking to her. Her heart fluttered and her stomach knotted at the realization.

Chapter Nine: A Step You Can't Take Back

"Lucy! What are you doing up?" Eleanor asked.

It was late. Eleanor had risen for a drink of water. Her daughter-in-law sitting at the kitchen table in the middle of the night had startled her. Lucy, meanwhile, had heard her come down the stairs and had quickly wiped her tears away on her sleeve.

"What is the matter?"

"I am sorry," Lucy apologized. "I didn't mean to frighten you. I couldn't sleep. I thought that warm milk might help."

Eleanor looked across to the stove and spotted the pot. The burner, however, was unlit.

"Let me do that," Eleanor offered. She walked over to the stove and lit the burner. She then regained her chair at the table. "Do you want to tell me what is wrong?"

Lucy buried her face in her hands.

"Has this got something to do with Andy?" Eleanor prompted.

Lucy looked up and nodded.

"I know that I am Albrecht's *maem,* but I also like to think of you as my *dochder,* so you can talk to me about what is bothering you. I promise that I will listen."

With a pained nod, Lucy collected herself. "When I decided to search for the sender of the *Grischtdaag* cards, I never expected this. I never expected that it would be Andy or that we'd become friends so quickly. I never expected that he would be so much like Albrecht. Sometimes I forget that he's not Albrecht."

The milk bubbled. Eleanor bolted to the stove and moved the pot. She poured the warm milk into two mugs and added a sprinkle of cinnamon before carrying them back to the table.

"So, is that what is wrong? You feel guilty for spending time with Andy?"

Lucy shook her head. Something she said sailed over Eleanor's head. Lucy struggled to find the words and hold back her tears.

"After Albrecht died, I did not believe that I would find someone else who understood me the way that he did. Then, I met Andy. When I am with him, I feel as though Albrecht is with me. I don't feel so lonely."

Eleanor sipped her milk. She let the silence linger. Lucy felt obliged to break the silence.

"I didn't expect it. I met with Andy to learn more about Albrecht, nothing more. I thought that a childhood friend could fill me in on what he was like before I met him. I was hoping to better know the man I had lost. Albrecht still holds my heart, but Andy..."

"You are conflicted?"

Lucy nodded.

"That is understandable," Eleanor said. "You've suffered much. Has Andy said anything to you?"

Lucy stared blankly at her mother-in-law.

"About his feelings?"

Lucy shook her head. Though Andy hadn't, she was terrified that he might. Either way would be cause for consternation; rejection, she feared, and love, she begrudged. The latter, however, hurt the most.

"*Gut*," Eleanor said. "Well, then perhaps you might take a break from seeing Andy again until you have had time to clear your mind and sort through your feelings. You want to be sure that you are not confusing comfort during grief with anything more. I would be delighted to reminisce about Albrecht's childhood with you."

Lucy nodded, if only to be left alone. She had hardly taken a moment to catch her breath since she had begun taking her daily walks with Andy. A step back to figure out her feelings may be the antidote to her fears. She did not want to hurt him nor to get hurt. Indeed, a break seemed like a sensible plan.

"You're right, Eleanor. I think I do need some time to clear my head."

"When are you seeing Andy again?" Eleanor asked.

"We planned to walk again the day after tomorrow."

Eleanor tapped Lucy reassuringly on the hand. "I'll ask Moses to have one of the farmhands deliver a message tomorrow to tell him you're unable to accompany him."

Lucy was grateful for the reprieve. It was a relief to her not to have to see Andy when she was this conflicted.

"It's late, and I'm getting cold," Eleanor announced. She arose, collected the mugs, placed them in the basin, then turned to Lucy. "Why don't we go on up to bed now and try to get some sleep?"

Lucy nodded. She wrapped her shawl tightly around her

shoulders and made her way toward the kitchen door. At its threshold, she turned.

"*Danki*, Eleanor."

"*Gaern gschehne*. Moses and I only want what is best for you."

Lucy smiled. "*Gude nacht*."

"*Gude nacht*," Eleanor echoed.

Lucy eventually made it into bed. It was cold, so she curled up in the fetal position. *It was not always like this,* she thought. *I used to have another with whom to share the bed and to keep me warm.* She sighed. Her lament went unbaptized, for there were no tears left in the weary soul. Her conversation with Eleanor replayed itself in her mind. Lucy did need some space away from Andy. Even so, should she see him again, she feared lacking resolve. His company soothed her. If she let on that she enjoyed his presence, if she betrayed her original intent for agreeing to meet with him and watch birds, she would be in the mire. It would only make matters worse. Thus, she decided to return to her parents. Albrecht was dead. A doppelganger, emotional or otherwise, would not fill his void. Her heart ached at the thought of leaving Eleanor and Moses, for would they not grieve all the more? Still, she would unravel if she remained. Her aching soul gave way to exhaustion and fell asleep.

Chapter Ten: Seams and Stitches

L ucy dreamed of skating on the lake. She was thrilled, happy, and secure. She awoke refreshed from the previous night and reached for the cards in her drawer. The winter scene on the lake held her attention, for it was where she had been in her nocturnal fantasy. Albrecht had visited her, if only by making his presence felt. She had not seen him. Her fingers traced the image. She smiled. Then she opened the card to read it, finally noticing the initial "A." *Albrecht didn't sign it,* she remembered. She shivered at the thought of who she'd really dreamed about. Her resolve to leave returned. Lucy had to inform her in-laws.

The morning passed slowly with Lucy dreading her announcement and what it would do to Eleanor and Moses. Breakfast had been consumed and cleaned up, morning chores were complete, and now the widow sat at the kitchen table pitting dates. A speech was forming in her mind. Lucy rehearsed it, then imagined the Yoders' dejection, and she despaired. Such was the morning's cycle. A knock at the door interrupted her. She wiped her hands on her apron and went to see who it was.

"Andy! What are you doing here?" As Eleanor had planned, Lucy had sent a message to the farm to say that she would be unable accompany Andy on his walk on the morrow.

Andy frowned. "I got your message. Still, I need to talk to you."

Lucy was coy. Home alone, she had no one to check her resolve. Eleanor was out visiting a friend. Moses was working on the farm. "I am preoccupied at the moment. Can you come at another time?"

"*Nee.* It has to be now."

Lucy stepped out onto the porch. After all, it would be inappropriate to have a gentleman caller in the home with no chaperone. She wrapped her arms around herself and rubbed them. "I'm listening."

Andy exhaled slowly. He seemed nervous. "I'm not sure how to say this." Andy licked his lips, looked around, then inhaled. "I think I just need to come right out and tell you."

Lucy knew exactly where this train was going, and there was nothing that she could do to stop it. "Andy!"

"Please, let me say it. I think that I am falling in love with you—"

"—I think you should go."

Their words overlapped, but Andy's were louder. Andy's had conviction, whereas Lucy's were frantic. Lucy had been afraid that this would happen, and now it had. She was too late. Lucy pursed her lips and looked down.

"Did you hear what I said?" Andy asked.

Lucy nodded.

Andy waited. Lucy avoided eye contact. The girl shifted. The cold was biting. Unwavering, Andy stood his ground, awaiting a reaction.

"I can't discuss this," Lucy offered.

It did not appease Andy. "I am not asking you to discuss

anything. I am just telling you how I feel."

"*Danki* for letting me know," Lucy said weakly.

Andy's furrowed eyebrows meant Lucy had not heard the end of it.

"Does this have something to do with what you told me on the night of the nativity play?" Andy asked.

"*Nee*," Lucy said. Then, to get out of the cold and away from Andy, she whispered, "It's too soon. I'm not ready for this."

Andy had not imagined that response in preparation for this confrontation. He felt guilty. With a hand behind his head and shifting his weight onto one foot, he apologized. "I don't mean to pressure you. You are still grieving Albrecht." He nodded. "I can wait. For however long it takes."

Lucy saw hope in Andy's face. That was not the desired outcome. She had wanted an end to this. He thought that what he was saying was the right thing. A simple *thank you* would have been enough. After all, his patience could hardly have been a bad thing. Lucy had slowly stitched herself back up, and Andy's friendship had helped to hold her together. Yet, with this loose string, she pulled it, loosening her fragile state. She said the wrong thing.

"I don't want you to wait. I won't ever be ready."

Andy's jaw was set. He was determined. He would not give up easily. Lucy had to use a one-two combo to push him away.

"You are not Albrecht, and I do not want to marry you." The jab had the desired effect; now for the cross. "I'm going back home."

Andy looked about to faint. "When?" he asked, hoping to call her bluff.

"Tomorrow. That's why I can't go on the walk with you."

Andy shook his head, refusing to accept Lucy's rebuff. "So that's it? You are just leaving?"

Lucy knew she had him. He was on the back foot. Now, the knockout. "Yes. There's nothing here for me anymore." The right words made one last dash to exit her mouth—the ones to say that he deserved someone who wasn't made up of crooked seams and dropped stitches, that he deserved someone whole and unbroken—but she shut her trap. A slight nod marked her farewell. She turned on her heel and hurried back indoors.

Andy stood on the porch, staring at the closed door, hoping it would open again. Surely Lucy could see that they had much in common. She had lost a part of herself when Albrecht and their unborn baby had died. Andy, too, was losing part of himself. They were perfect for each other. They understood one another. While they had not known each other long, he had never experienced such a profound connection with another. *Lucy must feel it, too*, he thought.

The door did not reopen, nor did the curtains pull back to see if he remained. Andy turned to walk the long road home. Her venom had numbed him. He walked feeling nothing, denying her departure, convinced that hurt people hurt people. The more distance he put between them, however, the more sting there was to the pain. *If only I weren't going blind,* he cursed to himself. *If only I were whole. Then she would see it!* Indeed, turning him away, Lucy had implied that Andy wasn't important to her. *"There's nothing here for me anymore."* Lucy's words replayed themselves over and over in Andy's mind. They drugged him, making him aimless in his step. He stopped when he heard the mourning dove. He stood on the edge of the lake where his hope for their love had first flickered and flamed like a candle in a dark room.

Andy sat on a snowy log, exhausted from his emotional burden. The snow glittered. The air was crisp. In his heart, it was winter, too. Without Lucy, it was cold and bleak like the bottom beneath. *Trust* Gott, he thought. *Let Him guide us.* He beckoned a lifetime of discipline to be calm. The calls of the birds, the creaking of the branches, the heavy snow sliding from the branches to fall with a *thud,* let him feel his despair and let it pass. The beauty of his austere surroundings comforted him. When the sun had reached its zenith, he arose to make his way to his family, the woman he loved having been pushed from mind and heart.

Part Three

Chapter One: The Unspoken Goodbye

Hope is hard to kill. Lucy Yoder closed the front door on Andy, literally and figuratively. Her words, presumably, had crushed him and dashed his dream of ever being with her. Lucy reflected upon all of this with her back against the door and Andy on the other side. *Could I be wrong?* she asked herself. *What if I'm right and there's no one left for me? What if he's heartbroken for the rest of his life?* Lucy could not decide which was worse: being loved by someone who disinterested her or losing a love interest. Refusing Andy may be the twilight of her love life, rendering her a widowed old maid. *Which is worse?* She sobbed. Her chest heaved. Her shoulders shook. She suppressed her cries with all her might.

"Lucy?"

Through blurred vision, Lucy made out Eleanor's silhouette before her. "I'm sorry."

"You needn't apologize to me, *Liewi*," Eleanor reassured. "Do you want to talk about it?"

Lucy shook her head. "I can't."

Eleanor made a sad duck face, tilted her head to the side, and rubbed her daughter-in-law's arm.

"Do you mind if I go to my room?" Lucy asked.

"Go! I'll be in to see you later," Eleanor said.

The cost of moving on seemed greater than the status quo. Oh! Would that it be easier to move on! Couldn't she just get over Albrecht? How did the other widows do it? Lucy regained her bedroom and threw herself upon her bed. Andy's dejected face haunted her in that position, so she turned to her back. There, up on the ceiling, she could imagine their first walk in the woods together, his joy in being with his crush. Lucy took a deep breath, closed her eyes, and exhaled. *I have to move on,* she thought. *I must move away.*

The late afternoon sun was streaming through the thin, cream curtains. Lucy sat up to look around the room. Her room had not looked as such when she first closed her eyes. *I must have slept,* she thought. A quick splash of cold water from her basin refreshed her but did nothing to wash away her feelings of helplessness and guilt.

Downstairs, Lucy could hear the low voices of Eleanor and Moses in the kitchen. She could picture them seated around the table, looking concerned and bewildered about how to help her. The guilt made her sick. Lucy had stayed on the Yoder farm to comfort Moses and Eleanor. Presently, however, she was a worry. *Yet another reason to go back home,* she concluded. Lucy stepped into the kitchen.

"You're awake," Eleanor said. "I checked on you a little while ago, but you looked so peaceful that I did not want to disturb you."

"I'm sorry that I did not help with the dinner," Lucy apologized.

"No matter," Eleanor assured her. "It's only soup and bread, nothing I couldn't manage on my own."

Lucy nodded, picked up her bowl and went over to the pot

resting on the stove. She ladled herself a small helping of the thick, vegetable soup. Upon regaining her seat, she noticed that both Eleanor and Moses had watched her every move.

"This soup is *gut*," Lucy said.

"It is," Moses agreed. "I think I will have some more." He rose from his seat and walked over to the pot.

Eleanor had not taken her eyes off Lucy, who avoided her gaze. She did not want to talk about Andy. She had nothing to say that would relieve their anxiety.

"Moses," Lucy said. "May I ask you a favor?"

Moses nodded as he sat back down.

"I have decided that I want to return home for a while. I was wondering if you might have time tomorrow to drive me."

Lucy's request took them by surprise. Neither of them spoke. Moses ate a spoonful of soup. Eleanor looked to her husband and played with her hands.

"Of course," Moses said. "I can take you after breakfast."

"*Danki.*"

Eleanor wanted more. "I didn't know that you wanted to go home." She interlaced her fingers.

Lucy looked into her bowl. "I haven't seen my parents in quite some time. I thought I would surprise them."

"They don't know you're coming?" Eleanor asked.

Lucy shook her head.

Eleanor looked to Moses, whose eyes were set on his food. She breathed quickly and played with her fingers. "For how long will you be away?"

"I'm not sure," Lucy admitted.

Eleanor frowned. Without eye contact, she was doomed to short answers and pithy words. She dropped her hands to her lap and bowed her head. The poor lady had resigned herself to the idea of losing her daughter-in-law. The only sound in the room came from the spoons that scraped against the bottom of the bowls. It reflected the disharmony in Lucy's mind.

That night, Lucy fetched her suitcase from beneath the bed. Opening it transported her back to when Albrecht had carried it for her when she came from her father's home to his as a new bride. She trembled. Her spasms were such that her hands could not clasp a thing, let alone fold and set her belongings in order. She inhaled—*Albrecht brought me here*—then exhaled—*Albrecht left me here.* She opened her eyes. *It's time to go.*

Lucy opened the wardrobe to collect her things. Albrecht's shirts and things hung in the same wardrobe though behind another door. Lucy made certain not to open the other door.

Breakfast that morning was a quiet affair. Eleanor, who was usually bright and cheerful, sat reserved, her face pale and tired. Lucy chewed on her toast and swallowed all that she wanted to say. Besides, the words wouldn't come out, for they were caught in her throat.

"We should get going when you're done eating," Moses said.

Lucy nodded and carried the empty dishes to the sink. As she washed them, Lucy resolved to make things right with Eleanor. However, Eleanor was gone, and the kitchen was empty. The message was clear to Lucy; Eleanor was too distressed and hurt to see Lucy go. The poor soul was losing the last remaining part of Albrecht the week before Christmas.

Lucy went to the buggy near the barn. The farmhands had come to say goodbye and to wish her a Merry Christmas. The back door slammed. Moses walked toward them carrying out what her groom had carried in not a year ago. He carefully lifted it and placed the suitcase inside the buggy.

"Are you ready?"

"*Ya*," Lucy confirmed. The farmhouse was lifeless. "Is Eleanor coming?"

Moses shook his head. "She wants to, but she can't."

Lucy had not wanted to make Eleanor feel as though she had lost yet another child. Still, she could not blame her. The cold made it difficult to swallow her despair. Lucy hated the thought of letting Eleanor down.

"Let's get going," Moses said, quietly.

Lucy nodded and climbed up onto the buggy. Moses picked up the reins, and the buggy set off. When they reached the edge of the Yoder property, Lucy turned to take one last look at the house that had been her only home as a bride and as a widow. She left her identity there. When she returned to her community, she would revert to being her parents' daughter, her year away more of a blip than an entirely new existence. It was at the Yoders' that she had fit into her new role in life. Her wedding night, her birthday, her first fight as a wife, her and Albrecht's first make-up as a married couple, long, balmy summer nights spent sitting on a blanket on the front lawn to gaze up at the stars in each other's arms. It had all happened there. Her time as a wife and expectant mother had lived and died there. Albrecht, too. The grief embittered the feast of her time on the Yoder farm —coriander upon a beef wellington; enough to be noticed, but not enough to ruin one's appetite. Lucy had wanted more at the gala, but alas, it was not only the fattened cow but also the cook that had been butchered. Lucy yearned for that feast, refusing to eat anything else. Thus, she was starving.

Nearer the road, Lucy suddenly spotted a pale, drawn face

in the front room window. Then the figure disappeared as if she'd never been there at all. Lucy closed her eyes. She was leaving her heart behind so that the rest of her could live.

Chapter Two: The Returning Tide

"**A**re you going on a walk today?" Andy's mother had made him a hearty breakfast of bacon and waffles.

"*Nee*," Andy said. He picked up his fork to dissect the waffle into bite-sized pieces.

Sarah raised her eyebrows but dared to say no more. Andy had been in a mood since returning the previous afternoon. Nothing could cheer him up. Andy ate despite his lack of appetite. This was comfort food.

"I was thinking of calling in at the Yoders' this afternoon," Sarah said. "It was so lovely to see Lucy the other day; I thought I might bake something and take it over to them."

"Lucy is gone," Andy said.

"Gone?"

"She went back home this morning."

Sarah frowned. "Did you know that she was going back?"

Andy shook his head.

"She didn't mention it to you?"

"Why would she?" Andy spat.

"Well, I assumed that you two were friends."

"We're not."

Sarah sighed. *As if my boy hasn't lost enough,* she thought.

"May I be excused?"

Sarah looked across at Jacob. He did not budge as though the entire exchange had escaped him. She nodded.

Andy took his cue and left. He escaped to the great outdoors. Its scents and air were all he could appreciate now that his sight was poor. In his haste to be rid of any thought of Lucy, he did not dress for the occasion. Such was his rage that the winter's breeze could do little more than cool him off.

The reality of Lucy leaving had sunk in upon telling his mother of the situation. His determination and resolve had sunk deep into the lake from where he had first perceived them. He was a child again, small and vulnerable. It was impossible for him to imagine a life without Lucy. With her, he had felt like he could amount to something, achieve more than the status of *blind man. What is she thinking about now?* he wondered. *Will she even remember me?*

∞∞∞

Naomi and Jeremiah Bontrager were surprised to hear a buggy pulling up outside of their home. No visitors were expected; they had planned to visit others instead. Surprise turned to delight when they caught sight of their daughter, Lucy, standing beside the carriage.

Lucy had not returned home without Albrecht. It was strangely familiar to see her without him. The last time they had seen their daughter had been at the funeral. Since then, only handwritten letters had been exchanged, and that sporadically. They had felt forgotten. Lucy, thus, seemed a familiar stranger to them. But she was home!

"Lucy," Naomi said, as she opened the door. "What a *wunderbaar* surprise! Why didn't you tell us that you were coming home?"

Lucy embraced her mother. "I only just decided; otherwise, I would have written to tell you."

Jeremiah hugged his daughter and then turned to Moses. "It's *gut* to see you."

"And you," Moses agreed.

"Would you like to come in for some *kaffi*?" Naomi offered.

"*Danki* for the invitation," Moses replied. "It is kind of you, but I must get back."

"There is never a moment's rest for a farmer," Jeremiah commented in understanding.

"This is true," Moses agreed. He then handed Lucy's suitcase to Jeremiah and turned to Lucy. "You are always welcome," he said quietly. "Should you wish to visit, our door is open."

Lucy's throat swelled. She forced a smile. "*Danki*," she whispered.

Moses cleared his throat and turned back to the Bontragers. "*Sehn dich widder* (See you again). *Frehlicher Grischtdaag* (Merry Christmas)!"

"*Frehlicher Grischtdaag*," Naomi repeated.

Moses climbed onto the buggy, tipped his hat, and picked up the reins. "*Kik-kik!*" The horses clip-clopped away up the muddy street. Lucy and her parents watched the buggy carry their daughter's old identity and life away until it was out of sight.

Lucy was not sure what it would be like to be back home. In some ways, it seemed as if an entire lifetime had passed since she'd been back. Lucy had grown up. She had been young, romantic, and hopeful. Now, she was a butterfly caught in a gale. She had only just gotten herself up off the mat.

"Why are you hovering at the door?" Naomi asked. "Come inside before you catch a cold."

Lucy stepped into the house and looked around. Everything was exactly the way it had been before she had left. The familiar brought little comfort. She had changed, but home had not. Would she still fit in? Presently, Lucy felt more stranger than kin in her own home.

"Would you like something to eat?" Naomi offered.

"*Nee, danki,*" Lucy said. She was drained from the morning's emotions. "I think I will unpack."

"Come downstairs when you are done," Jeremiah instructed. "We would like to hear how you've been."

Lucy nodded, took her suitcase from her father, and went to her small bedroom on the eastern side of the house. She hesitated at the door. The last time she had been in her own room was on the morning of her wedding. Albrecht would not be on the other side. Nor would her *newehockers*. She had since taken everything from there and moved. *This is not a new beginning,* she thought. Her hand gripped the doorknob such that her knuckles turned white. *I want something that isn't here,* she thought. *So, why am I here?*

Lucy opened the door. The room was unchanged from when she'd stepped out as a blushing bride. It smelled musty. Whatever part of her that had been there was long gone. Lucy pulled back the blinds, opened the window, and let the winter air refresh the place. She closed the door. There, hung a blue dress, cut plain and simple. She put out her hand to feel it between her fingers. It was real. This was the dress she had worn the last time she'd been in this room. It had been a church dress and a birthday dress until Albrecht had passed. Lucy had since been unable to look at the dress. Since it would have been wasteful to throw the dress away, Lucy had done the only thing that she could think of and had sent it home. She had expected that her mother would pack it away.

Lucy touched the soft material and was returned to her wedding morning. She and her *newehockers* had giggled and chatted as they dressed. Nerves and excitement had possessed the bride. Presently, those feelings came back to her though they were as foreign to her as Bulgarian cuisine.

"How do you feel?" Hannah had asked, her eyes shining.

"Filled with the light and love of *Gott*," Lucy had said. She had beamed with said light. How fortunate she had felt to have met a godly man who wished to be with her 'til death.

"*Gott* is *gut*," Hannah had agreed. "You and Albrecht are perfect for one another."

Lucy's face had already hurt from smiling, but she had not cared. Hers was a bright future in the arms of a faithful Amish man. Her face was going to hurt for years to come!

Lucy's hand dropped to her side. She turned away from the dress. The memories stabbed at her heart, causing it to leak anything good and true and worthy. Soon, she would be destitute of joy and exultation. Home was supposed to be an escape from grief, yet there she was, marinating in it. Lucy placed the dress in the back of her closet to be kept out of sight. She quickly closed the door to pack away her troubled emotions, too. Lo! Such things are not on rods but cling only to the heart.

Lucy's stay in her parents' home was currently one of reminiscence, when in fact, she'd come to plan her future. Her mind struggled to remain present. To distract herself, Lucy helped her mother bake Christmas cookies, kept busy with the usual chores, and wandered about her old stomping grounds. Nothing worked. Distance, then, was not the antidote to Andy and the Yoders.

Though calm, Naomi had little patience for her daughter's sluggish ways in the kitchen. Her confrontation was blunt and to the point. "You seem distracted. Is there anything you want to talk about?"

Lucy shook her head as she removed a tray of *pfeffernusse* cookies from the oven. "I am fine, *danki, Maem.*"

"*Nee*, you're not. You can't tell the difference between a quarter cup and a quarter teaspoon. I ask you for the sugar and you pass me the flour. I asked you to set the oven and you put on the kettle! *Liewi*, tell me what's wrong?"

Lucy shrugged and blushed. Knowing what this meant, Naomi cut to the chase.

"Will you go and visit Hannah? Perhaps you might take her some cookies." Indeed, getting her daughter out of the kitchen was the best things for Naomi's nerves...if they could finish a good batch!

Lucy nodded. It was only a matter of time until Hannah learned of her return. One could not disappoint a close friend at Christmas.

"*Ya*, I will," Lucy said.

Naomi looked pleased. "I will prepare a basket for you." In doing so, she found some cheese and other cold snacks to share. "You go and get ready. I'll finish the cookies."

Lucy smiled. "*Ya, Maem.*"

Naomi made quick work of the cookies with her moping

daughter out of her hair. She fed the family lunch, then set Lucy on her way. Peering through the kitchen window, she watched her daughter walking down the street. It had come as a shock that Lucy was as morose now as on the day of the funeral. That was unexpected. Albrecht had died in the late summer after mere months of marriage. They had not had a chance to develop the deep love of decades. *Surely Lucy should have moved on by now,* Naomi thought. *What's holding her back? Dear* Gott, *help Hannah get it out of her.*

Hannah and Lucy had been childhood friends. When Hannah married an Amish farmer from a neighboring *gmay*, they'd moved out of town. Her letters to Lucy let on that she was pleased with farm life and married life, too. A sign at the fork in the road pointed to the Mast farm. Lucy stared at it, then took the opposite road.

Lucy had intended to see her friend, but the closer she got to the house, the more she realized that she could not bring herself to knock on Hannah's door. Hannah was happy and married. Lucy was jealous. She could not in good conscience go to Hannah's house and pretend otherwise. At present, it was best to stay away.

The houses and buildings disappeared. Land opened up before her. Lucy looked across the gray hills and fields. *Does Hannah's place look like this?* she wondered. She tightened her shawl around her shoulders. An imaginary conversation with Hannah ensued in her mind.

After Albrecht died, my grief was an ocean. The waves lapped at my mouth and nose. I was certain that I would be swallowed up by the waves and disappear into the abyss. Yet, something changed at the beginning of December when I received those Christmas cards.

(She said it as though Hannah already knew what she was talking about) *It felt as though the tide had turned. I could wade out of the water. But I didn't want to. The water was familiar. Albrecht was no longer on the beach. I thought that coming here would take me out of the waves and into the woods. But that's not what happened. Instead, since coming home, the water keeps rising. I feel trapped.*

Lucy's friend understood, hugged her, told her all the encouraging words she'd wanted to hear, all in her imagination. Thus, there was no reason to visit Hannah. Lucy had gotten what she'd wanted on her walk. She returned home, set the basket down, and panicked. How would she explain the undelivered basket?

"Lucy? Is that you?" Naomi asked.

"*Ya, Maem.*"

There was a knock at the door.

"Will you see who that is please, Lucy?" Naomi asked.

"*Ya.*" Lucy opened the door to find her father standing on the porch with a surprise visitor.

Chapter Three: A New Life

"Thomas!" Lucy exclaimed.

"*Gude daag*, Lucy," Thomas replied.

Lucy was taken aback. She had no words for this surprise. Before her stood her first crush, and he seemed far more attractive than he had in her memories. A statuesque six-foot-two frame crowned with brown locks, equipped with the shoulders of a bison and a chest fit for King Kong, towered over her. His emerald-green eyes beckoned her gaze, and they disarmed her. Indeed, they could have opened the vault to Fort Knox with a mere glance. He was beautiful, pretty, almost. His countenance was far more captivating than Lucy had ever imagined. Thomas Smucker, childhood friend, classmate, and love interest had not visited since his *Rumspringa*. And then it dawned on Lucy why she couldn't tear her eyes away from him: he had not grown his beard! The way Lucy saw it, there was something about a clean-shaven man that contrasted with an Amish one: his bare face was this Amish girl's eye candy. No whisker hid his square jaw, nor did it hang over his chest, obstructing the view. Lucy's heart fluttered such that she unwittingly fanned herself. Thomas smirked. He knew he had her.

"Would you like to come in?" Jeremiah asked.

"Only if it's no trouble, Mr. Bontrager," Thomas replied.

"Of course, it's no trouble," Jeremiah insisted. "Please, come inside."

Thomas obliged. Lucy needed a moment to let him pass. She was unwilling to leave the candy shop yet. Jeremiah cleared his throat. Lucy backed away, allowing her father to show him into the sitting room.

"Take the seat by the fire," Jeremiah instructed Thomas. Then he turned to Lucy, who was still enamored by their guest. "Lucy, please tell your *maem* that we have a visitor."

Lucy nodded.

"Who was it?" Naomi asked, looking up from her pot bubbling on the stove.

"It's Thomas Smucker," Lucy said.

Naomi did not seem in the least surprised that he had called. The lady moved into action. "I'll put on some *kaffi*. Why don't you go back to the sitting room? Tell your father to come help me. You two can catch up."

"I can help make the *kaffi*," Lucy said defensively.

"I can manage," Naomi insisted as she shooed Lucy toward the door.

Lucy was pushed out of the kitchen, but she kept looking over her shoulder, trying to convince her mother that she could let the men alone. It was then that she noticed her mother already had out all that she needed to serve her family and a guest laid out on the counter. Giving in to her mother was a stock reaction for the shy girl. Obediently, she returned to her father and Thomas in the sitting room. Jeremiah sat in the old hickory rocking chair by the window while Thomas sat across from him next to the fire. Only one other empty chair had been set, and it was near the guest. The conversation was about some new farm equipment that Thomas's father had recently purchased.

"It's cut down our harvest time by half," Thomas said, sounding quite the salesman. "It was a fine investment."

"That's *wunderbaar*," Jeremiah agreed.

Lucy sat down and listened politely. Like most girls, she could feign interest in farm equipment about as well as she could sing baritone in a barbershop quartet. Her father, however, was feigning. He hadn't the slightest interest in farming. He didn't even garden for a hobby. His specialty was commerce. That was his trade. He cared if he could sell it, not about the latest ways to make it. If he had a hobby, it was smoking the pipe. Nevertheless, he behaved the way others did around the Smuckers. Theirs was a well-to-do Amish family. It did not matter how often they gave away their wealth, their land remained the most productive in the county. Coupled with their business acumen, the Smuckers could be wealthy Amish despite their *Ordnung* forbidding luxuries. Like the rhythm of the seasons, the Smuckers made money, were deemed to have too much by their elders, gave it away, and began the cycle anew. Thus, they were prominent, revered, and reviled. Lucy and Hannah had thought that Thomas was supercilious. They had teased him so when they were girls.

"How is your *daed*?" Jeremiah asked.

"He is well," Thomas replied. "As healthy as a horse, he tells me, but I think he's getting ready to hand over the reins to me."

"Well, why not? What are *seh* for?"

Just then, Naomi entered with a tray of coffee and Christmas cookies.

Thomas arose to greet her. "Mrs. Bontrager, it's *gut* to see you."

"And you, Thomas," Naomi replied. "What a pleasant surprise."

"Well, when I heard that Lucy had returned home, I couldn't help but to call," Thomas said. He glanced at the widow.

Something's afoot, Lucy thought. She smiled politely. His looks were keeping her off-balance. She resigned herself to enjoying her treat presently and inquiring about her misgivings later.

"How is your family?" Naomi asked.

"They are all well, *danki,*" Thomas replied.

"*Gut,* well you must be sure to send them our best wishes and *Frehlicher Grischtdaag.*"

"Of course."

Naomi poured the coffee. "Lucy baked the cookies." She let Thomas have first pick of the batch.

"Well, then, I will be sure to have at least three," Thomas promised.

Naomi and Jeremiah both smiled. Lucy, however, gazed at him straight-faced. She did not like being tricked, but she detested a scene. Thus, she sat quietly, smiling now and again. Thomas continued to chat all about himself, his family, his future on the farm, his health, and how he'd returned to the faith upon an extended *Rumspringa.* "It's what I know best," he said. He tried to entice Lucy into the conversation, but her shyness was a natural conversation killer.

"Still the shy one," Thomas chided.

Naomi had a bright idea and spoke up. "Why don't we leave you two to catch up? I have some things that need doing in the kitchen."

"And I must get back to the store," Jeremiah said. "With

Grischtdaag just around the corner, there is always someone needing some or another forgotten ingredient." He rose. "It was nice to visit with you."

"Well, it was a pleasure to see you both again," Thomas said.

"And you," Naomi said. "I will be in the kitchen if you need anything."

"Please come again," Jeremiah said.

Lucy's parents vacated the room, leaving the childhood friends alone.

"I must say, Lucy, it is awfully *gut* to see you again."

Lucy smiled politely and blushed.

"When I heard that you had come back, I wanted to rush right over here, but my *maem* advised against it. She said that I should give you some space and let you settle in."

Lucy frowned. "Why?"

"Why, what?"

"Why did you want to come around so urgently?"

Thomas's thick eyebrows knitted together. "You are serious? Surely you know how I feel about you, how I have always felt about you! When I heard you had gotten married, I was devastated."

Lucy stared.

"I know it was probably presumptuous of me, but I thought that after I returned home from *Rumspringa,* you and I might take a buggy ride."

Lucy stared at Thomas. It was as if he'd been living in a parallel universe to hers. She had teased him as a boy! Surely he did not think that she had feelings for him! "We hardly knew each other when we were younger."

"What do you mean? We've known each other our whole

lives!"

Lucy sighed. "I don't feel like I know you."

"Well, why don't we rectify that?" Thomas asked. "How about a buggy ride with me?"

Lucy looked frightened by the proposition.

"Please," Thomas said. "Just think about it?"

Lucy did not wish to take a buggy ride with Thomas. She knew, however, that he did not hear the word "no" very often. Thus, she would have to stall. "I will think about it."

Thomas seemed satisfied. He sat back in his chair and helped himself to another cookie.

Her senses returning to her, Lucy set about a trap. "How did you know that I had returned?"

"Your *maem* sent a note," Thomas blurted.

Lucy was speechless. Inside, she was aghast! How could her mother encourage a suitor at a time when she was so vulnerable? *It's not his fault,* she reminded herself.

"Thomas?" Lucy's tone was steady. "I will think over your offer to join you in a buggy ride. Now, I've chores to attend to." With that, Lucy rose.

Thomas did not do so immediately. He looked to her, smug, grinning, confident. It did not, however, aggravate Lucy. She'd been married. She may still be a teenager, but pain had numbed her passions while simultaneously sharpening her nostalgia. She smiled back, just as smugly.

I'm gonna get you, Thomas thought.

I'm gonna get my parents for this, Lucy thought.

Thomas left. Lucy collected herself, then headed to the kitchen to confront her mother. Perhaps her father would get involved. *Surely he would not approve,* she thought. *What on earth was she thinking, sending him that note!* "*Maem*! I need to talk to you."

"Yes, Lucy. What is it?"

"Why did you send a note to Thomas letting him know I was back in town?" Lucy said it with a tremor in her voice.

"Well, can't a *maem* help her *dochder* plan her future? You don't want to remain a widow forever, do you?"

"I am a widow now, *Maem*. I am not ready to forget Albrecht. And when I am ready, I will not choose Thomas." Lucy nearly choked saying his name.

Mother was annoyed at her daughter's sharp tone. "That's enough, Lucy. Things have been difficult for you, and for that, we are sorry. Still, as your parents, we want what's best for you."

"Being set up with Thomas Smucker is not what's best for me," Lucy interrupted.

"Neither is being alone," Naomi quipped. She slammed her kneaded dough on the table the same way she beat her carpet. "We have missed you. We were happy for you to live away with Albrecht and the Yoders, but your time with them is now over. You are home now, amongst your kin. We would like you to stay and to choose a suitor from our *gmay*. That way, you can raise *kinner* here where we can share the joy of them. Would you not want us to see you and our *kinskinder*?"

"I did not stay away to hurt you," Lucy declared.

"Nevertheless, your decision to remain at the Yoders' after Albrecht's death was not easy on your *daed*. Or me." Naomi picked up her dough and kneaded it anew. "I am asking you, Lucy, to please consider Thomas. He comes from a *gut* family, and he would treat you well."

"I don't know, Thomas," Lucy insisted.

"You didn't know Albrecht, either!" Naomi seethed. "Get to know him." She roughhoused the dough. Beating it was all that stood between mother shaking the sillies out of daughter. *Why can't children listen to wisdom?* Naomi thought. *Why must they argue? It shouldn't be this hard to talk sense into them!*

There was no point in arguing. After all, it was the child who was the widow. The elder woman had not loved and lost. *She'll never understand,* Lucy concluded. "I told him that I will think about taking a buggy ride with him," Lucy said.

Naomi exhaled, then nodded, satisfied.

"But I made no promises," Lucy added.

The dough continued to suffer Naomi's ire.

"I'm going for a walk," Lucy announced.

"Don't be too long. It's almost time to prepare supper."

Lucy walked to the back door, opened it, and hurried outdoors. She sprinted through the yard to escape both her past and her future. Sobs for Albrecht cascaded from her tender eyes; weeps of self-pity drowned her hope. She gasped for air. *A mourning dove!* Lucy hastened toward it.

Naomi shook her head, sighed, and put supper to the fire.

Chapter Four: The Fork in the Road

"Let's take a walk this afternoon," Sarah Peachey suggested.

Andy was seated in the old rocking chair on the porch. Christmas would be upon them in a few days, yet the weather was mild, pleasant even.

"Andy? Did you hear me."

Andy turned his head slightly to peer over his shoulder at his mother who was standing in the doorway.

"It's a beautiful afternoon," she said. "We could go to the lake."

Andy was angered by the attention and that he did not have a good reason to refuse his mother's offer. He did not want to go walking. He wanted to wallow. His mother asking him to walk to the lake to forget the one that got away was the irony of ironies. Still, his lament would make him fit in among the fishermen. "I just want to sit on my chair and be left alone."

"I am worried about you. You haven't been yourself these last few days. I think a change of scenery will do you some *gut*."

"Fine," Andy spat. His mother being right harmed his self-pity. If she had it her way, he'd be over Lucy by Christmas Eve and no relatives would have to know about his broken heart.

"I am just about to put lunch on the table," Sarah said. "We can go afterward."

Andy said nothing. His mother retreated into the house. After lunch, Andy and Sarah set off toward the lake. Andy offered nothing by way of conversation. Silence enveloped them until the lake came into view. Sarah reached for Andy's arm.

"I wanted to talk to you away from the house," Sarah said.

Andy frowned. She did not continue. His blood boiled. *What's she up to?* he wondered.

"I know that something is wrong. And my instincts as your *maem* tell me that it has something to do with Lucy's departure."

Andy opened his mouth to argue, but Sarah raised her hand to indicate that she hadn't finished.

"I'm sure that you don't want to talk about it, but you would feel better if you did. There is no one around here but me, and I promise you can tell me anything. After all, a problem shared is a problem halved." Sarah smiled to her only begotten.

Andy made her wait. He looked out across the lake. He shifted his feet. He inhaled. He exhaled. He reminisced about a time when he believed that his parents could fix anything, and he took his time, too. Decency eventually won him over, prompting him to think of what to say, how to explain himself, and how to express his feelings. Indeed, saying the words aloud would be cathartic.

Andy replayed his and Lucy's episodes: the funeral, the lake, the nativity. "I told Lucy I loved her," Andy confessed, "and she rejected me." *Of all the places to begin*, he cursed himself.

Sarah hid her shock about as well as a sapling hid a rhino. "Did you mean it?" she blurted.

Indignant, Andy replied, "Of course! Why do you think it hurt so much?"

"I'm sorry," Sarah apologized. "I'm surprised, that's all."

"It came as quite a surprise to me, too."

Sarah was at a loss. Andy had been so quiet on the way over, then he'd just spilled the tea. Without warning. The discomfort of silence now seemed like a bed of roses. Sarah panicked. *I have to keep him talking, but how?* she wondered. "Did you believe her?" That was her best shot.

"She was pretty convincing," Andy deadpanned. He made his way to the lake, hoping to escape the jaws of his mother's inquisition.

Sarah had other ideas. She hurried to catch up with her son. Grabbing his arm, she swung him around. "Andy!"

"What do you want from me?" Andy snapped.

"I want you to face your feelings about what happened."

"I know what happened," Andy cried. "She did not want to be tied to a man who is going blind. Can you blame her? I don't want to live with myself. Why should she? She's lost a whole man; why would she settle for half of one? You see me: I can't do anything right. *Daed* doesn't want my help on the farm anymore. I can't steer a buggy. I can't see the birds anymore. I can understand why she doesn't want me around. My own *daed* doesn't want me around." Andy was screaming.

"Did she say that? Did she say that she did not wish to be with you because of your condition?"

"Not those exact words, but I am no fool, *Maem*. I told her how I felt, that we had much in common, that we understood each other. Still, she rejected me."

The force of Andy's double rejection now hit home for Sarah. Her family was wrenched apart because of a genetic condition. Her boy had grown up, but he would never see it. *How can*

I make him see it? she wondered. The questions, sometimes, are the answers.

"You are kind and compassionate. You are loyal, considerate, and tough." Sarah choked back tears. "These are *gut* qualities. They touch the heart and make us feel vulnerable. That's when they can intimidate us. You won't quit even when your eyes do! You can see people. You empathize. You've done so since you were young. That's why you made the cards for Lucy.

"How did you know about those?" Andy was more mortified than embarrassed. He still feared Amish legality and its consequences. What if his mother told on him?

"I have eyes, Andy. I can see through floors."

Andy smiled and shook his head. *What a relief!*

"You saw Lucy clearly, at least in the beginning. You saw she was hurt. She was alone. After all, living with your in-laws is hardly the place to grieve. Somewhere along the way, you stopped seeing her so clearly."

Andy was on the edge of his seat. "Go on."

"With what?"

"What am I supposed to do?" Andy was pleading.

"I don't know, *Liewer*. I didn't invite you here to lecture you. I brought you out here to listen."

"I don't know what you want from me."

"What did you see that last time you looked at her?"

"I don't know." Andy looked at his mother.

Sarah raised her eyebrows.

"She was hurt."

Sarah's gaze unnerved him.

"She seemed hurt," Andy stammered.

"Mm-hmm," Sarah said. "Go on."

Andy thought. His mind's eye retained its twenty-twenty vision. "She was uncertain. She lacked conviction." He looked to his mother as though he'd made a discovery. "She was scared."

Sarah nodded. She waited a beat to let Andy's revelation sink in. "I think that Lucy's reasons for leaving may not be the ones you believe them to be. Grief has a way of twisting people out of shape."

A mourning dove cooed.

Andy remembered Lucy wrapping herself in her shawl as though she were trying to keep it together. *Had she feared coming undone before him? Why?*

"Over the last year, you've been handed more challenges than most people face in their whole lives," Sarah continued, softly and slowly so as to compliment rather than interrupt her son's thoughts. "You've handled your grief and loss with courage and grace, which is rare for someone so young. You're unique, Andy. She knows that. Those who have experienced loss pray to *Gott* for help while they swim in a sea of emotions. If they can't bury it, they run."

"Is that what Lucy is doing?" Andy mused. "Is she running away?"

"Perhaps," Sarah said. "She might be afraid of falling in love again."

Andy stopped walking. His mother was right. Moreover, when he had confessed to Lucy that he was falling in love with her, he'd done so without taking a moment to consider how it would make her feel. The days which they had spent together had made him brazen. He'd forgotten how fragile Lucy was. That's when he'd lost sight of her. His proclamation had frightened her delicate soul. This epiphany transformed his mood. He felt guilty, the need for confession, and hopeful all at once. It was repentance and forgiveness that would set things right. *And patience,* Andy told himself. *Love is patient.* Imbibing this information lightened his head, making him giddy. *There's still a chance.*

"What should I do?" Andy asked.

"I can't tell you what to do, but I will tell you where to start: a little tenderness would be helpful."

Andy nodded, hand on chin.

"I am proud of you, Andy. You are a fine young man."

Andy froze. "I wish *Daed* thought so."

Sarah sighed. "Your *daed* is grieving, too."

"Why? I'm not dead."

"*Nee,*" Sarah agreed, "but the *buwe* he knew is gone. He is grieving the *soh* he'll never have. Give him time. He'll see you for who you are."

Andy nodded. But he had a more pressing issue at hand. His relationship with his father was a battle for another day.

Sarah perceived that her son was burdened by life, love, and longing. She remembered something she'd done when he was a child. Gott *be thanked,* she told herself. "I wonder if, before we return home, you'd like to hear a story."

"Don't you think I am a little old for your stories?" Andy said, trying his best to be polite and keep his concentration.

"Not this one," Sarah said. "I've been saving it for when you get older. It's the story of your *groossdaadi's* painter's box."

Andy nodded and said, "Oh!" A mystery solved would be a welcome reprieve.

"It's not your father's favorite story, which is why he isn't here to hear it," Sarah cautioned. "Still, I think that you might understand yourself better once you hear it."

"I'm listening, *Maem*."

Sarah looked out across the lake to gather her thoughts. She inhaled, then began. "When your *groossdaadi* Eli's eyesight was so bad that he became housebound, I would sit with him. He'd talk until he felt he had been heard. Then, there was peace. It's hard to see the light leave someone's heart. Talking helped him to navigate what was happening to him. He would question *Gott's* will openly, then submit to it. Don't forget, Andy; our *Gott* is not a fragile *gott*. He can take our hardest questions and our fiercest critique."

Andy remembered coming in from the farm to find his mother and grandfather on the porch chatting. It had not occurred to him, however, that his grandfather's failing sight had caused a crisis of faith. He'd taken his grandfather's steadfast faith for granted. Knowing he was not alone in a struggle gave Andy comfort and rekindled hope.

"When Eli was a child, before he understood the proper ways, he loved to draw. He would draw on stones, in sand, with chalk or charcoal, and unlike the scribbles of other small children, his drawings were clear, delicate, and advanced beyond his years. Upon discovery, his parents forbade him from ever drawing again. Instead, he was told to concentrate on his chores. His father was a stern man, so any rebellion on the part of Eli was quashed. Your *groossdaadi* conformed to the life in which he'd been born. He confessed to me that he did his best to be a *gut soh* but when alone, he would tear paper from his lesson books and draw in charcoal. He would draw scenes of trees, birds, *Grischtdaag* festivities, and portraits. Then he would hide the drawings underneath a loose floorboard in his room."

Andy smiled. It was strange to think of his mischievous

grandfather. The old man had been dignified. *How did he hide it so well?* Andy wondered.

"Your *groossdaddi* had a secret plan," Sarah continued. "When he turned sixteen, he journeyed to the city for *Rumspringa*. He went to the Goshen College to try to study art. He begged for an audience with the dean of the school. You can probably guess how his parents reacted. It caused quite a scene!"

"But what did the dean say?" Andy asked.

"He was a kind man. He gave your *groossdaadi* his choice of medium. Charcoal is what he chose. Then, he was given a sheet of paper upon which to draw. The dean observed his work. It took ten minutes to convince him. He'd never witnessed such raw talent. Your *groossdaadi* was offered a scholarship."

"He went to art school?" Andy was incredulous.

"He did. While there, he met a girl named Rose. She was an art student as well, and she was talented and gentle. They became friends. Not long after meeting her, your *groossdaadi* planned to ask Rose to marry him. They had wanted to travel to all the great art capitals of the world together, but before he had a chance, a great sadness struck. The vision of your *urgroossvadder* began to fail, and fast! Your *urgroossmudder* begged your *groossdaadi* to come home. He did, shattered like a clay pot. He returned to the farm, never to leave again."

"What happened to Rose?" Andy asked.

"He left her behind," Sarah said. "She was part of the life he had lost. Your *groossmammi* married him and raised a family with him. But he never lifted a pencil or paintbrush again."

"But what about the box?" Andy asked.

Sarah inhaled. "It was a gift from Rose. A constant reminder of what could have been. He hid it in the basement."

"Do you think he ever forgot about it?"

Sarah shook her head. "That box symbolized a time of great joy that, as far as I could tell, he mourned to his dying day."

The reality of his grandfather's lost future stirred the grandson. "*Groossdaadi* chose the farm over painting due to his failing eyes. As for me, the farm has essentially been taken away from me for the same reason." The thought lingered.

Andy's beloved grandfather had chosen to leave two loves behind and return home. Andy's decision was nowhere near as difficult. The choice was to add to his life, not trade one thing for another. He did not have to choose between his family and the woman he loved.

"The footsteps of *Groossdaadi* are not the ones I wish to follow. I'm going to talk to Lucy."

Sarah nodded. "I thought you might."

Chapter Five: The Lie

Andy held tightly onto the reins of his horse. It trotted along the unfamiliar dirt road. Never had he thought of controlling a steed again since Buddy, nor had he ever been so brazen as to take a mount without his father's permission. Yet, there he was, compelled by love, trusting the eyes of a beast to lead him to his beloved.

"Are you sure you don't want to wait until after *Grischt-daag*?" Sarah Peachey had asked.

Andy had shaken his head. "I must go now. It can't wait."

Sarah had not argued. Instead, she had prepared him lunch. Her son was starved for love; he would not be starved of bread on his journey. Andy gave his mother a kiss on the cheek, then mounted the mare.

He'd traveled for two hours, finding no signs indicating the Bontrager house. Andy contemplated knocking on someone's door. A figure walked his way, so he decided to ask him for directions.

"Excuse me, I was wondering if you could help me," Andy ventured. "I'm looking for the Bontrager house."

A boy lifted a finger and pointed the way. "It's just up the road and to the left. It's the house with the green roof and the squeaky porch swing."

"*Danki,*" Andy replied. "I am grateful for your help."

The boy nodded. Andy proceeded up the road until he reached a large white house with a green roof and a porch swing. He stopped and dismounted. "You wait here, girl," he instructed as he looped the reins through the white picket fence.

Andy opened the small gate. A shiver of nerves and apprehension greeted his entrance into the yard. Head spinning, he wondered what he was doing there. His feet carried him up the narrow path to the porch and halted. There was a squeak. Someone was sitting on the swing. It was a man, looking away from Andy and down the road, perhaps daydreaming. Andy figured that they were around the same age. Lucy had no brothers. Perhaps he was a cousin visiting for Christmas?

"*Gude nammidaag,*" Andy said politely.

The man jolted. "*Gude daag!* Why, I didn't see you there. Who are you?"

"Is this the Bontrager home?" Andy asked.

"*Ya,*" the man confirmed, "but they are not home. I was just waiting for them myself."

Andy nodded. "I am Andy Peachey."

"Thomas Smucker," the man replied.

Andy looked up and down the porch. "Do you mind if I wait? I've come a long way."

Thomas shook his head. "Not at all! Please, sit."

Andy sat down on the swing. He then remembered his lunch. Eating might pass the time and distract him from his nerves. "Would you like half a bologna sandwich?" Andy offered.

"*Nee, danki,*" Thomas replied.

"Would you mind if I ate?"

Thomas shook his head. "Go right ahead."

Andy retrieved his lunch from his saddlebag. Thomas watched with great interest. It was clear that the man was partially blind. Andy returned to his seat, opened the brown bag, and discovered something extra that his mother had packed: an envelope and a pen. There was a note attached to the outside of the envelope in his mother's handwriting.

In case you can't speak the words that your heart wishes to say.

Andy opened the envelope. Inside was a card he'd painted on the night of the school's nativity play. When Lucy had left, he'd thrown it away. His mother had rescued it.

"Are you a relative of the Bontragers?" Thomas asked.

"*Nee*, I am just an old friend. What about you?"

Thomas chuckled. "Not yet, but I soon will be."

Andy frowned. He fixed his gaze upon the man as if to say, *What do you mean?* Thomas felt obliged to explain.

"Lucy and I are old friends. We were at school together. Now that she has returned, I have asked her to marry me."

"You and Lucy are a couple?" Andy stammered.

"*Ya*," Thomas said.

Andy's mind was reeling as he stared into the smiling face of this stranger. Before he knew what he was doing, Andy stood up and began to run toward the gate.

"Are you leaving?" Thomas called after him.

Andy did not answer. He threw the gate open, unhooked the reins from the fence, and mounted the horse. "*YA!*" The horse made haste in the direction from whence they'd come.

"Whoa, girl," Andy said. As the mare skidded to an abrupt halt, he pulled the pen and card from his bag, inhaled deeply, then wrote in the card. Once finished, he slipped the card into its envelope and turned the horse around. He returned to Lucy's home and placed the Christmas card on the mat.

"What is that?" Thomas asked.

"It's a *Grischtdaag* card," Andy explained.

Thomas nodded. "You're not staying?"

"*Nee*, I need to get back home. When you see Lucy, will you tell her that I came by to say *Frehlicher Grischtdaag*?"

"*Ya*, of course," Thomas promised.

"*Danki.*" Andy regained his horse and left without once turning to look back. His last goodbye was sealed in the envelope that now sat on an old woven doormat.

Chapter Six: The Last Card

"Thomas? What are you doing here?" Lucy had not yet promised him anything, so he was unexpected. She'd just returned from the store where her parents were taking inventory before closing up for the Christmas holiday.

Thomas arose from the porch swing and stepped toward Lucy. "I was waiting for you," he said.

"Why?"

"I thought we might take a walk."

"I've just walked from the store." It did not surprise her in the least that Thomas had sought her out.

"Don't tell me that you weren't planning on walking this afternoon. The weather is perfect." Thomas was right. They had been blessed with an extended autumn. The afternoon was warm and bright.

"If it makes you feel better, I promise to walk on the other side of the road; that way we might as well be strangers headed in the same direction."

Despite her feelings about Thomas, Lucy smiled. "If you wish to walk in the same direction as me, I can't stop you. After all, it is a public road."

"Shall we go, then?"

"I need a minute," Lucy said. She wiped her boots on the doormat before stepping inside. The door remained open. Thomas watched her walk down the hallway carrying her basket of supplies, turn to the kitchen, and disappear out of sight.

Lucy had not seen or spoken to Thomas in two days. Despite her mother's wishes and pleading, Lucy was disinterested in Thomas. It seemed, though, that he was unwilling to reconcile himself to that fact.

"Do you need any help?" Thomas called from the front door.

"*Nee, danki,*" Lucy called back. "I'll be right out."

Thomas kept his word and walked on the opposite side of the road. There was nothing strange or unfamiliar about his behavior toward her. Thomas was intent on filling every silence with talk about himself.

"I've spoken to my *daed* about buying some more land and extending the farm," he said. "He thinks our property will be too big, but is there such a thing? I told him that I have plans for a larger home, one in which to raise many *kinner*. My *fraa* can have all the space that she needs to sew and to cook. I can farm even more acreage and increase our pastureland. The cows will have the best milk in the county!"

It was evident that Thomas did not require Lucy's input to continue the conversation. He was doing quite well monopolizing the talking. Thus, she let her mind wander. The glistening snow and then the birds caught her eye. The sun's rays peeking through the leaves streamed onto her and her boredom, so they played peek-a-boo. A mourning dove joined in nature's symphony.

"Lucy?" Thomas called. "Did you hear me?"

"Mmm," Lucy lied.

"Then, it's settled. I will pick you up on the day after *Grischtdaag*."

"For what?" Lucy asked. She turned to look at Thomas and spotted something sticking out of his pocket. Her heart stopped beating. "What is that?"

Thomas frowned. "What is what?"

"In your coat pocket!"

Thomas looked down to see a corner of Andy's envelope was sticking out. "Oh, it's nothing." His eyes betrayed him.

"Thomas," Lucy said through gritted teeth, "what's in your pocket?"

Thomas sighed and removed the envelope. Lucy recognized the familiar, slanted writing on the front.

"Someone left it on your doormat."

"Who?" Lucy demanded.

"I don't know," Thomas said. "I didn't recognize him."

Lucy felt her heart pounding as she stretched out a hand toward Thomas. "Give it to me."

Thomas hesitated. Lucy's reaction had confirmed his assumptions that what he held was more than a mere Christmas card. "I don't think it's a *gut* idea."

Perplexed, Lucy stared at him, disbelieving what she'd just heard.

"Your *maem* told me that you were trying to move on from the past," Thomas explained. "Perhaps you should let this go."

"Thomas! Give me the card."

The chastened child handed the card to the motherly figure lest he be spanked. Lucy quickly unsealed the envelope and removed the Christmas card. The painted scene was of a young couple seated on an old stone wall looking up at the starry sky.

With hands trembling, Lucy opened the card.

Lucy,

There were many things that I wanted to say to you—things for which I needed to apologize and others that I wished to confess. As I write this, I regret having waited so long to come after you.

I don't want to stand in the way of your moving on. I will, however, continue to believe that Gott led me to you under the silver maple tree. I will cherish that day. Here was a gott who saw your pain and knew mine. In His wisdom, He decided that we would do well to be in each other's lives. It was not in the way I'd hoped. Nevertheless, I will ever be grateful to Him for allowing me to be a part of your story, even if it was for just a little while.

Take this, the last of my Grischtdaag cards, and be merry. Be joyful, Lucy, and find love again.

Frehlicher Grischtdaag.

Your friend always,
Andy

Lucy's world ceased to exist except for the words before her. There Andy sat, in her mind's eye, bewildered and disheartened, composing his grand finale after having painted her most vulnerable moment. Such compassion! Such delicacy! Such tenderness! And how had he gotten it to her? He would have had to travel for hours!

"Lucy? Are you all right?" Thomas asked. He could see that she was moved, blubbery-eyed, and grieving. "I knew this was a bad idea." He shook his head.

Lucy's eyebrows furrowed as she stared at Thomas. A controlled rage bubbled within her. *How did Thomas come into posses-*

sion of this card? she thought. "Tell me the truth, Thomas. If I had not seen this card in your pocket, would you have kept it hidden from me?"

"To protect you? *Ya.* Your *maem* is right, Lucy. You need to move on with your life. I am serious when I say that I want to create a future with you."

Nearly knocked out by the utter stupidity of Thomas's illogic, Lucy did not know where to begin. She stared, hoping that the words would find her. Thomas took it as his cue to resume his favorite topic: himself.

"You've lived too long with your grief, and it's time to start planning a life again," Thomas continued. "Can you imagine the kind of life we might have together on the farm where we will raise a *familye* and our *kinner* can grow and flourish under *Gott's* great sky? I am a *gut* man. I will be a great *mann.*" He continued speaking, but Lucy had tuned him out. *Andy came here to give this to me. He did this for me. I want this!*

"Thomas! I'm not sure what my future holds, but what I am certain of is this: I do not want a future with you."

"And why not?"

"Because I don't love you."

Thomas scoffed. "Love! I can give you more than love! Love is a mere feeling. What I can provide is a life, a home filled with *kinner*, and a place to grow old. Is that not love? And more?" He paused to let the vision develop itself in Lucy's mind. "Do you really think the man who wrote you that card can offer you a better life than I can?"

"This isn't about him," Lucy said. "I don't believe that you've ever loved someone more than yourself, Thomas, for if you had, you would know that it is a gift from *Gott.* You would not speak of it with contempt. You don't love me. You want a *fraa*. I am not that woman."

Thomas shook his head. "You are making a mistake walking away from me."

"I am uncertain of a great many things, Thomas Smucker, but walking away from you is not one of them." Lucy turned on her heel and walked home.

"You've already had one great love in your life; do you truly believe that *Gott* will grant you another?" Thomas called after her. "Do you think there is another who would want you?"

Lucy did not answer, nor did she turn. She clutched the card tightly in her hand. From behind, Thomas could not tell that he had struck a chord. Lucy paled at the thought: had *Gott* given her another great love? And had she chosen to let him go?

Chapter Seven: Strangers

Lucy returned home. She pushed open the front door and heard her mother calling from the kitchen.

"Where have you been?"

"I went walking," Lucy replied.

"It was quite a walk!" Naomi said.

Lucy nodded. She eyed her mother. There was something about the way she was looking at her that made Lucy suspicious. "Do you wish to ask me something?"

"I was just wondering if you had any company on your walk today."

"I should have known," Lucy exclaimed.

"I saw Thomas in town yesterday," her mother said. "I may have mentioned that you liked to take walks every afternoon."

Lucy shook her head. "*Maem*, this has to stop. I have no interest in creating a future with Thomas."

"But if you'd just give him a chance, who knows?"

"I did give him a chance, and he was juvenile! We had a frank discussion this afternoon when I told him that I do not wish to marry him."

Naomi shook her head. "Mary and I can make this right. I'll speak with her."

"You're not listening to me! I don't want you to talk to Mrs.

Smucker. I don't want anything more to do with that family. I am not marrying him!"

"Why are you sabotaging yourself?" Naomi asked. "Don't you want more than this?" She pointed to her daughter in the same way she'd signal a pothole in the road.

Lucy shook her head. "Marrying Thomas will not *fill* this!"

Naomi looked lost. She was searching for words, searching for the daughter she knew, and looking for her place in her world. "I used to know how to help you," she whispered, "but I don't know who you are anymore."

And so, mother finally came to terms with the reality set before her. Lucy had made her own way. Naomi had nothing to do with it. They were strangers now, seated at the kitchen table. Thankfully, their need to prepare for dinner guests kept them occupied for the rest of the afternoon.

The Bontragers entertained relatives for supper. It was then that Lucy smiled for the first time all day. She glanced across the table at her mother. The cracks between the two needed mending, but it would have to wait until after her aunt, uncle, and cousins had left.

"*Maem*," Lucy said, "will you go for a walk with me?"

Naomi nodded. They set out along the road that seemed like a dock heading to sea because of the fluffy clouds sailing overhead. The moon shone brightly.

"Did you really mean what you said?" Lucy asked.

"I wish that I hadn't said it," Naomi confessed.

"*Nee*," Lucy replied, shaking her head. "It's okay."

Naomi sighed. "Everything happened so quickly. From the moment you met Albrecht, it felt as if our family had been engulfed in a whirlwind. Your love for him was all-consuming.

You'd finally found someone, and we were happy for you, but it was difficult to watch you leave home with ease."

Lucy frowned at the memory of how she'd behaved. As soon as Lucy had met Albrecht, she had become so caught up in him that she had hardly given anyone else a thought. She could empathize now.

"We were devastated when Albrecht died," Naomi continued. "You were inconsolable. We spoke to you, but we had no idea if you heard us. It was like talking to a shadow. You have no idea what it is like for a *maem* to see her *dochder* in such pain and not be able to do anything." Naomi blubbered, using her shawl to wipe away the tears.

Try as she might, Lucy could not recall her parents' presence at her side. Her only thoughts had been for the deceased —Albrecht—again, commanding the entirety of her attention even in death.

"When you did not want to return home with us, that was hard. Hannah told us how you felt about leaving Albrecht's parents, but we needed you, too. We were in pain, too, Lucy. You are our *dochder*. Who would be better than us to help you? Them? The Yoders?" Naomi huffed. "Your *daed* and I prayed to *Gott* that He would look after you and comfort you. We missed you so much!" Her grief once again got the better of her, so she hid her face in her shawl.

Lucy felt stupid for not realizing how her actions had impacted her parents. She had been enshrouded in her own grief. *I was a bad daughter,* she admitted to herself.

"I was so happy to see you home," Naomi continued. "*Gott* had answered our prayers! You had returned to us. Still, you were suffering. I tried to help you. I truly believed that meeting someone new might bring back the *dochder* I once had." She sighed. "I was wrong, and now I've pushed you further away."

"*Nee*," Lucy said. "That's not true. I'm standing right here. I hear you, *Maem,* and I'm sorry. I never meant to cast you aside. I thought that I was doing the right thing!"

"We never blamed you," Naomi said, gently. "We just missed you."

"I missed you too," Lucy confessed.

Lucy caught a song in the breeze. She craned her ear to identify the bird. She then found it sitting on a fence post to confirm. "It's a Red-breasted Nuthatch," Lucy whispered, not wanting to scare it.

Her mother looked amazed. "How do you know?"

"A friend taught me," Lucy explained.

Naomi looked at the little bird. Lucy placed her hands in her pocket to keep warm. There, she felt the Christmas cards.

"Can I tell you a story?" Lucy handed her mother the cards.

Naomi looked up from the cards and nodded. For the next hour, mother and daughter walked along the side of the road, all but abandoning the evening's preparations for the following morning. Lucy told her mother all about the Christmas cards and their sender, the confusion about their signatures, and how Thomas had lied about the last one. She left out no details, and her mother listened without interruption. It was Andy who'd taught her about the birds, she finished.

"And these walks made you happy?" Naomi asked.

The simple question choked Lucy. She had not yet confessed her great fear of losing another great love. She coughed, hoping it would loosen the words from her soul. She nodded. She coughed again. Finally, she uttered, "They brought me peace."

Naomi nodded. The pair made their way home, quietly. Mother had noticed something profound in her daughter. However, she would not pry. Lucy had said much to clarify what had happened. Upon reaching the front door, Lucy threw her arms around her mother to hug her. There they stood until their teeth chattered.

"I was about to send out a search party!" Jeremiah teased.

Mother and daughter smiled at each other.

"We had a lot to talk about," Naomi said.

"Care to fill me in?" Jeremiah asked.

"How about I make us some tea?" Lucy offered.

"That would be *wunderbaar*," Naomi agreed.

Lucy bolted to the kitchen. Naomi marched to her room to change. Jeremiah was left wondering if he'd said something wrong.

Lucy went into the kitchen, made the tea, then carried it to the living room. Naomi had regained her husband's side by the fire. Andy's Christmas cards lay open on the coffee table. Their art was gorgeous by kerosene lamp.

"What's going on?" Lucy asked.

"You're *maem* was telling me about these cards and about the young man who sent them to you."

Lucy nodded.

"Do you love him?" Jeremiah asked.

The question threw Lucy off balance, so much so that the tray teetered in her hands. The question came with more force from her father's mouth. He rose quickly and took the tray.

"Please, sit," Jeremiah said.

Lucy did as she was told while Naomi moved the cards to one side. The tea was set, and Jeremiah poured.

"Looking at these *Grischtdaag* cards, it's clear that he is in love with you," Jeremiah continued.

"He is," Lucy said. "He told me right before I left."

"Yet you still left?" Jeremiah asked.

Lucy shook her head. She lowered her gaze to her lap where she played with her fingers. "It's not that simple." Lucy smiled, shyly, hoping to bring an end to the subject.

"Enlighten me," Jeremiah said.

"I am not sure if I am ready for love again."

"*Gott* seems to think otherwise, Lucy," Jeremiah said. "He has a hand in everything we do. If He has directed this young man into your life, do you not believe that it is a *gut* and precious thing?"

Lucy looked from her father to her mother. "I feel guilty because I still love Albrecht."

"You will always love him, *Liewi*," Naomi said. "There's room in your heart to love another, one who's alive."

"I also worry about what Eleanor and Moses might think."

"You won't know until you speak to them," Jeremiah said. "They are *gut* people. I trust them to understand."

Lucy's mind raced as she considered all that her parents were saying. "So, what should I do?"

"Your heart will tell you. Listen to it," Jeremiah instructed.

"But I can't go back!" Lucy objected. "I've just returned home."

Lucy's parents merely looked on as though waiting for her to make the right move. Lucy clicked her tongue.

"I want to go back and speak with Eleanor and Moses," Lucy said.

Both Naomi and Jeremiah smiled.

172

"I will take you in the buggy first thing tomorrow," Jeremiah promised.

Lucy looked at her parents and smiled. The joy of her decision welled up within her to escape down her cheeks. Her heart swelled. She cocked her head forward and interlaced her fingers, unable to wipe the smile from her face. This was it. This was the magic and joy of Christmas.

Chapter Eight: Home Again

Lucy and Jeremiah set off early on Christmas morn. The journey was bumpy yet still. Only the birds were about this yuletide. Butterflies fluttered around in Lucy's stomach. For a shy woman, seeking her in-laws' blessing was a daunting task. She was afraid to be unclear and thereby lose esteem in their eyes.

"How are you feeling?" Jeremiah asked.

"Slightly apprehensive," Lucy admitted. "When I left, Eleanor was upset with me. I have no idea how she will feel now that I've come back to seek a blessing for leaving again."

"Well, there is nowhere to go now but forward," Jeremiah said.

Lucy smiled. Her father had always been a glass-half-full type of person. She just wished that she'd inherited more of his optimistic demeanor. As they moved further away from Lucy's childhood home, she replayed the conversation she had had with her mother before they left.

"Are you sure that you don't want me to stay?" Lucy had asked.

Naomi had taken Lucy's hands in hers. "I'm sure. You need to go back to move forward."

Lucy had wanted to reply, but the lump in her throat had

muted her. They had only just begun getting to know one another again. Why must life be full of constant change?

"I do want you to make me a promise," Naomi had said.

"Anything," Lucy had said.

"You'll make the journey home once a month to come and see us."

"Every other month," Lucy had countered. "I want for you to come visit me, too."

"*Gut*," Naomi had said, smiling. "Then I can let you go knowing that it's only goodbye for now. *Sehn dich widder*."

"I love you," Lucy had said.

"We love you too."

Lucy had hugged her mother tightly, hoping that the hug said everything that she could not. It was mid-morning by the time the buggy stopped at the Yoder farm. Lucy hesitated as she looked across the garden at the farmhouse.

"Shall we go inside?" Jeremiah said.

"*Ya*," Lucy answered. She climbed down from the buggy and followed her father toward the house. Just before they reached the porch, Lucy heard the familiar creak of the front door opening. There stood Eleanor and Moses Yoder.

"Well, look who's back," Moses said. "It must be a *Grischtdaag* miracle!"

Lucy's eyes were focused on Eleanor who had yet to say anything.

"*Frehlicher Grischtdaag*. We're sorry for the short notice," Jeremiah apologized.

"Not at all," Moses said. "You are always welcome in our home."

Jeremiah smiled his gratitude.

"Please, come inside," Moses offered. "We will have some *kaffi*."

Moses turned and Jeremiah followed him inside. However, neither Eleanor nor Lucy moved.

"Eleanor," Lucy began.

"Why have you come back?" Eleanor asked, cutting Lucy off.

"I made a mistake," Lucy confessed. "I never should have left the way that I did, but I was confused, and I'm sorry I hurt you."

Eleanor's hands trembled. "You broke my heart when you left." Eleanor's voice wavered. She sniffled.

"I am so sorry," Lucy apologized again.

The two women looked at one another, Lucy waiting for her cue. Eleanor finally opened her arms and embraced Lucy. "I've missed you," she murmured into Lucy's hair.

"Me too," Lucy whispered.

Lucy and Eleanor remained entwined until Moses had decided it was enough. He cleared his throat, and they finally let go.

"I'm sorry to interrupt, but I promised Jeremiah a cup of *kaffi*, and I'm afraid I might set the kitchen on fire," Moses joked.

Eleanor rolled her eyes. Lucy giggled, her nerves billowing from her belly to her throat and out of her face. Her entire being quaked. The nerves were gone. Another Christmas miracle!

"Don't you dare set my kitchen on fire!" Eleanor warned over her shoulder. "I'm coming."

Moses disappeared. Eleanor said to Lucy, "We can chat when the men have settled in the sitting room."

Lucy nodded and followed Eleanor into the house.

"Goodness, gracious, my *mann*, it's as simple as boiling

water!"

The quartet settled into the living room to warm up and enjoy their yuletide java. Once seated, there were the usual pleasantries about health and farming, Jeremiah's store, and the latest gossip. Lucy could see, however, that both Eleanor and Moses were wondering why she had returned.

"This is *gut kaffi*," Jeremiah said.

"*Danki*," Eleanor replied.

"We are glad to see you, Lucy," Moses said, marking an end to the customary greetings.

"I am glad to see you both too," Lucy replied.

Moses set his empty mug onto the table and sat back. "When you left us just before *Grischtdaag*, you seemed desperate to return home. Yet, here you are. Did you forget something?"

"*Nee*," Lucy smiled, appreciating his humor. She inhaled, then began. "I made a mistake in leaving. I do not regret going home because I was able to gain some perspective with the help of my parents as well as reconnect with my *maem* because our relationship needed mending. However, I realized that I was running away from my past. I was running away from how I felt because I feared what you might think."

"And what is that?" Eleanor asked.

Lucy hesitated.

"Go on," Jeremiah encouraged. "You can tell them."

"I want to live here, in this *gmay*," Lucy continued, "and I want to marry Andy Peachey."

The room was still. Only the flames dared to move. Moses and Eleanor looked at Lucy in stunned silence.

"I know that this may seem surprising to you," Lucy said. "It was surprising to me, too, at first to realize how I felt."

"What made you come to this realization?" Moses asked.

"Andy came to see me," Lucy confessed, "at my parents' house."

"He did?" Eleanor gasped.

"*Ya*, yesterday. However, I did not see him." Lucy reached into her pocket to retrieve Andy's latest card. She handed it to Eleanor. "He left it for me on the porch."

Eleanor and Moses read the card.

"I don't understand," Eleanor said. "This card is his good-bye."

Lucy smiled. "It was this card, Andy's goodbye, that made me realize I didn't want our story to end."

"Have you seen Andy yet?" Eleanor asked.

"*Nee*," Lucy said, "not yet."

Eleanor looked relieved. Lucy frowned. She had been worried that Eleanor's feelings toward her and Andy had not changed.

"You do not want me to marry him?" Lucy asked.

Eleanor sighed.

"I've known Andy his whole life, and he is a *gut* person," she said, "but I worry that marrying him will mean you become his nurse, not his *fraa*."

"Eleanor!" Moses exclaimed.

"Please let me finish. Lucy, you are a kind, warm, and compassionate young woman who's faced many hardships. If you marry Andy, you'll find yourself dealing with even more loss and pain."

"I appreciate your honesty, and I know you want the best for me," Lucy said. "However, if it is the will of *Gott*, would you still hold to what you've said?"

Jeremiah raised his eyebrows. Lucy was bold to corner such a formidable woman. Eleanor was speechless.

Lucy continued. "I know that this is *Gott's* plan. Andy knew it long before I did. *Gott* brought him into my life, and I began to live again after we lost Albrecht. He is the reason that I saw beauty and wonder in the world after everything had turned gray. I will always love Albrecht, but he is gone. I will obey my Lord and move forward."

Lucy's speech was followed by silence. She looked from one to the next to gauge a reaction. Moses spoke first.

"Are you sure?"

"I am," Lucy said. She cleared her throat.

"Then you should tell him," Moses concluded.

"*Danki*," Lucy said. "You have no idea how much your blessing means to me." She looked across at Eleanor who had said nothing. Jeremiah held his peace. Besides, his daughter already knew what he thought. Lucy got up and walked to where Eleanor was sitting. She squatted before her and took her hands in hers.

"Eleanor?" Lucy whispered. "Please, say something."

The older woman exhaled shakily and tightened her hands around Lucy's. "The day that Albrecht brought you home was one of the happiest days of my life because I could see how much you loved my son. I have loved you for it since." Eleanor's voice trembled. Lucy blinked back tears.

"Ever since Albrecht died, I've only ever wanted you to be happy again. It's not right that your love should have died with Albrecht because it's too precious. If you wish to give your heart to Andy and render another mother-in-law joyous, I will not argue."

"Are you sure?" Lucy asked. "Because I could not bear it if

you didn't mean it."

"I still have reservations," Eleanor confessed, "but I will not stop you if you believe that this is *Gott's* plan. I love you, Lucy, and so I will support you." Eleanor sniffled, then rubbed her eyes.

"I love Andy," Lucy said.

"Then he is a fortunate man," Eleanor declared.

Chapter Nine: My Heart

"**A**re you sure you don't want to wait until tomorrow?" Eleanor asked. "You must be tired from the journey and all the excitement. Besides, it's *Grischtdaag!*"

Lucy smiled. She had missed Eleanor's mothering. "There's no better time than this to surprise him!"

Eleanor ceased arguing. Instead, she put her hands on Lucy's arms. "You know that no matter what happens, you will always have a home here with us."

Lucy smiled, gratefully. "I should go," she said and headed out the front door. As she walked toward the Peachey farm, she tried to plan what she was going to say. Her mind was scattered, however. Should she begin by confessing her love? By correcting Thomas's lie? By thanking Andy for the card? She needed it to be perfect, but no matter what words she chose, nothing seemed right. Time was short. The farm was upon her. *Perhaps Eleanor was right,* Lucy reasoned. *Perhaps I should wait 'til morning.* She placed her hand on the Peachey fence to steady herself. She turned around to head home. Then, someone inside her possessed her. She was seething. "Don't be a coward," she muttered under her breath. "Just tell him you love him."

Lucy balled her hands into fists and returned to the fence.

She walked quickly up to the farmhouse. A loud knock at the front door let all inside know that she was there. It was unrecognizable, for she was still possessed by the bolder version of herself. Her presence would be unknown until the door opened.

"Lucy!" Sarah said, amazed. "What are you doing here?"

"*Gude daag*, Mrs. Peachey," Lucy said. "I am sorry to show up unannounced like this, but I was hoping that I might be able to speak with Andy."

"He's not here," she said.

Lucy's shoulders slumped. Her old self returned.

"Don't worry," she said. "He's just out for a walk; he shouldn't be too long. Do you want to come inside and wait?"

"*Nee*," Lucy said. "I would rather go and look for him."

"Do you know where to look?" Sarah asked.

"I have an idea," Lucy said over her shoulder. And she was off, hurrying back down the porch steps. Her manners returning to her, she turned to say, "*Frehlicher Grischtdaag*."

Sarah Peachey still stood in the doorway, astonished. "And to you," she called back.

Lucy smiled and ran toward the lake. A light dusting of snow covered the way. The lake was deserted. There were no signs of Andy. She had been so sure that he would be there.

"Lucy?"

Lucy turned. He *was* there. Andy stood, his coat and hair delicately frosted, cheeks pink from the cold.

"Andy! I am so glad I found you."

"What are you doing here?" Andy's tone was cold. Lucy shivered, frightened that rejection loomed. She had hoped that he would be happy to see her. Instead, he looked puzzled and annoyed at the mystery of her presence.

"I was looking for you," Lucy said. "I went to your house, but you weren't there. Your *maem* told me you'd gone out for a walk. She asked me to wait inside, but I figured you'd be here, so I came."

Andy shook his head. "I don't mean what are you doing at the lake. I mean what are you doing *here*?"

Lucy frowned. "I thought that you'd be happy to see me. It's *Grischtdaag*."

"*Ya*, well, I'm not," Andy said bluntly.

Lucy shook her head. "I don't understand."

"Did you get the card?" Andy asked.

Lucy nodded. She reached for it and pulled it out of her pocket.

"That card was my goodbye to you," Andy said. "So, I don't understand why you've bothered to come back *here*."

Still not having recovered from the icy welcome, Lucy stammered and stuttered, raising and lowering her shoulders, cocking her head, and moving her lips without uttering a sound. Unwilling to wait for her response, Andy turned to walk toward the woods.

"Wait!" Lucy called after him.

Andy did not stop. Lucy accelerated. "You said that we were friends."

Andy whirled around to face her. With a set jaw, he spat, "I said those things because I was trying to be the better person. I was trying to put a peaceful end to our story, though, now, I am regretting what I wrote. I should have been honest with you."

"What?" Lucy was near tears, her eyes seeking the man she'd known on Andy's face. He could not be found. He was stone.

"I'm talking about how you stood there and told me that you weren't ready. That you never thought you'd be ready. You told me that no man would ever compare to Albrecht. Then I find out you're engaged. It's clear, now, that you just didn't want to be tied to a blind man."

Lucy's eyes widened. "I'm engaged? Who said that?"

"The man on the porch swing told me."

"Thomas?"

"You could have just told me that you didn't feel the same way," Andy said, ignoring Lucy's question. "You could have told me the truth. I could have taken it. If you had, it would have saved me a lot of time and heartache."

Lucy shook her head, crying, disbelieving. "*Nee!*" was all she managed.

Andy shook his head. "I looked like such a fool, offering him half a bologna sandwich when he was probably laughing at me behind my back."

"What did he tell you?" Lucy insisted, hoping Thomas had not said what she feared he'd said.

"That he was becoming part of the family," Andy said. "That you were getting married. I still can't believe I came after you." Andy was animated, pacing with his fists clenched. His jaw was still locked.

"He lied!" Lucy shouted. "Thomas lied. I never agreed to marry him. I told him *that day* that I would never marry him. He kept your card from me. He hid it in his pocket. If I hadn't seen it, he would have thrown it away, and I would have never known!"

"Why would he say that?"

"My *maem*! It was her. Thomas is from a well-to-do family, and she thought that he might be a suitable *mann* for me. She wanted me to marry someone from our *gmay* so I wouldn't leave again. She was misguided, but her heart was in the right place, and to be fair, she didn't know that I was already in love with someone else."

Andy frowned.

"I didn't run away because I didn't feel the same way as you did. I ran away because I did and I was afraid. I know what it's like to have loved and lost; I didn't want to go through that again. So, I ran away, thinking that if I removed myself from this place, I could distance myself from the love I have for you. I was wrong. It followed me home. No matter how hard I tried to fight the feelings, they grew stronger. I am tired of running, now, Andy Peachey."

Prettier than any birdsong was his name on Lucy's lips. Andy closed his eyes to savor it, letting a myriad of emotions fight for position across his face. In his heart, he was joyous!

"I'm sorry, Lucy, but I can't do this again," Andy announced.

Lucy's heart hit the snow. "You don't love me anymore?" she whispered.

"I do love you, and that is the problem. I showed my feelings for you twice, and both times, I got my heart shattered into a thousand pieces. I've managed to put myself together, but I don't think that I could do it a third time. I don't think that my heart will heal again."

Lucy blinked back tears. "I'm sorry that I hurt you."

Andy nodded. "I understand why you're so afraid of love. If you choose love, then you have something to lose."

"So, I guess this is goodbye, then?" Lucy asked.

"I guess so," Andy agreed.

Lucy reached up and gently kissed Andy on the cheek.

"Goodbye," she whispered.

Lucy wrapped her shawl around her body as she turned around to walk away. It was the only thing holding her together. Andy watched her go until her figure disappeared into the woods. He turned away from her to walk in the opposite direction. The snow had stopped. The sun was shining. Everything glistened. It was the perfect late Christmas morn. Andy strode quickly to put as much distance between him and Lucy as he could. On the eastern side of the lake, Andy stopped walking to listen. Snowfall had a magical way of muting nature, then restoring its volume once it stopped. Crows and ravens cawed, redbreasts and sparrows sang, but his heart ached. That meant he'd heard the familiar sound of the mourning dove. He waited for it to coo again. When it did, it was directly above him. *You swore never to follow in your* groossdaadi's *footsteps,* he told himself. *You were not to suffer a lost love like he had.* "What am I doing?" Andy muttered.

Lucy walked to the Yoder home. She'd walked it a dozen times before, treading the same path, yet this time, she felt lost. Part of her wanted to keep walking and never return. However, she owed too much to her parents and Albrecht's to fall apart once more. She needed to hold herself together.

What will I do? Lucy wondered. *I can't stay here. I can't go home. Thomas won't give up.*

"Lucy!"

The wind howled, whirling sand, grit, and the little bit of snow that had fallen into the air.

"Lucy!"

Dear Gott! she prayed, *show me the way. I need Thee, oh! I need Thee.*

The wind died down. A redbreast called.

"Lucy!"

Then a mourning dove.

"Lucy!" Andy shouted, racing toward the girl.

Lucy turned around.

"Stop! You took something of mine," Andy panted.

"What?" Lucy asked.

"My heart."

Lucy shook her head. Then she giggled.

"That was cheesy," Andy said, sheepishly placing his hand behind his head.

"I like cheesy," Lucy said.

"I'm sorry for what I said. I didn't mean it. I don't want you to go, I don't want that card to be our goodbye. I have to live out the words I spoke to you before. 'There is no happiness in life without loss and hurt.' I will bear whatever loss and hurt life may throw my way for just a moment of happiness with you by my side." Andy stepped closer. Lucy gazed at him, doe-eyed. She could see the snowflakes on his eyelashes. "I love you, Lucy."

Lucy opened her mouth to respond, but Andy's lips snuffed her reply. The mourning dove ceased to coo. The Northern Cardinal called, ending in its customary *rrrrrrrr*.

Chapter Ten: Young and Happy

The January landscape was desolate and snowswept. The new year had brought in winter with a vengeance. The night had been white, but once the snow stopped, the mercury plummeted. Still, the ground's white blanket of virgin snow contrasted well with Lucy's second blue dress.

"You look lovely," Naomi said.

Lucy turned away from the window and smiled.

"*Danki.*"

"Are you ready?" Naomi asked.

Lucy nodded. "Ready."

After their kiss on the snowy road after Christmas, Lucy and Andy had returned to the lake to spend the remainder of the afternoon talking, planning. There was no time to waste. They wished to be married.

"We shall have to wait until spring," Lucy had reasoned.

"Perhaps not," Andy had countered, thoughtfully. "I will ask permission from the bishop to be married in the new year. Since this is your second marriage, and since we want a small ceremony with just our parents, he should be willing."

Lucy liked the idea of a small wedding, but she did not want Andy to miss out. "Wouldn't you like a proper wedding? After all, you've never been married."

"As long as I get married to you, I don't care who else is there."

"Well, then, if the bishop agrees, let's get married in the new year."

"I shall go and find him right now," Andy had said before rising.

Lucy had giggled and held him back. "Maybe wait until the morning?"

The sun had been low in the sky. Another Christmas was ending. That year, however, Andy had gotten the greatest gift of his life.

"I didn't realize it was so late," Andy had said. "Come! We should get you home."

The couple had returned to the Yoder farm. Eleanor had been standing on the porch, anxiously scanning the horizon. Upon noticing them, her anxiety had been replaced with delight. Andy had left Lucy at the gate with a promise to return on the morrow. Lucy had reached out to him to squeeze his hand before hurrying up to the porch.

"I'm so sorry!" Lucy had apologized. "Time ran away from us."

Eleanor had been smiling. "It went well, then?"

"*Ya.* It went well."

"*Gut.* Now let's get in from the cold, and you can tell us all about it." Eleanor had placed her hand around Lucy's shoulders to guide her indoors. It would not be long before she would cease to be her mother-in-law.

Andy had risen early the following morning to call on the bishop.

"I am sorry to come so early," Andy had said.

"It's no bother," the bishop had assured him. The short, balding man with the build of a wrestler and a grip that could make a horseshoe cry showed him in. "My door is always open. What can I do for you, Andy Peachey?"

"I would like permission to get married in the new year."

"Someone wishes to marry you?" The bishop had waved his hand and shaken his head. "I beg your pardon; that came out the wrong way." He'd cleared his throat. "Who will be the bride?"

"Lucy."

"Lucy Yoder?"

"*Ya*. We wish to be wed."

"I did not know that you two were a couple."

"It's a recent development. We believe that this is *Gott's* plan for us. We would like to get married as soon as we can and begin our lives together.

The bishop had seemed amused at the thought. He, of course, knew Lucy's story—and Andy's—though how Lucy and Andy's story had escaped him, he could not fathom. He had taken his time to choose his words carefully so as to avoid another slip up. "She knows about your condition?"

"*Ya*, she knows." Andy had averted his gaze. He hadn't planned for an inquisition on his health. *Gott's plan* had been, in his eyes, sufficient. Was the bishop stalling?

"Andy, why does she wish to be married here? Don't her folks want to host it?"

Andy had to think quickly. "Her folks are here for the holidays. Plus, the Yoders have been hosting her since Albrecht—since the summer. Since we're all here..." Andy had shrugged, letting his words hang in the air.

"That soon?"

Andy had nodded.

The bishop had looked impressed. Then he'd grinned from crow's feet to crow's feet. "You've had quite a *Grischtdaag*, haven't you?"

"*Ya!*" Andy had replied abashedly.

The bishop had eyed the man, nodding his head, smiling, then shaking his head as though trying to make himself believe what had happened. "Very well. If your folks confirm what you have said, I shall marry you both at the Yoder farm on the first Tuesday of the new year."

"*Danki!* I must go and tell Lucy." Andy had hurried out of the bishop's home and into daylight.

He had barged into the Yoder homestead and yelled, "Lucy! Lucy!"

Lucy had emerged from the kitchen, her hands covered in flour. "What's the matter?"

"The bishop will marry us on the First Tuesday of the new year!" Andy had proudly announced. "We are going to be *mann* and *fraa*!" Andy had grabbed Lucy around the waist and lifted her in the air.

"Put me down," Lucy had squealed. Try as she might to brace herself otherwise, she had been unable to keep her floury hands off of him. Her delicate handprints had decorated his coat lapel akin to Tibetan cave art.

Eleanor had come to the door. "What on earth?" Eleanor had exclaimed.

Andy had quickly put Lucy down on the floor. "I'm sorry, Mrs. Yoder. I got carried away."

The couple's flushed, smiling faces had lifted the woman's heart. Her time for mourning had passed. There was new life in the winter. *This is how young people should look*—Eleanor had thought—*happy, joyous, and excited for the future.* "Come on inside, Andy," Eleanor had said. "I'll make you a cup of tea."

Epilogue: An End in Sight

The doctor was dressed in a stiff white coat that rustled every time he moved. It was the only sound in the room. "Young man," the doctor chastised, "you are fortunate that your wife brought you here when she did."

Andy shifted in his seat and swallowed hard. Pride was the most difficult thing to go down, worse than fear, more bitter than bile. He pawed at his collar and scratched at his vest, sleight-of-hand to mask the source of his discomfort.

The doctor looked up from the file on his desk. "If your condition had progressed, say, another month, I couldn't have helped you. As it stands, photocoagulation should give you considerably better vision and stop any further deterioration for the next five to ten years. You'll still need reading glasses, but you'll see again."

Andy nodded.

"Andy? What do you think?"

Andy sat, stunned.

"Andy?"

"Sorry. I am still trying to process exactly what Dr. Robbins said."

"He said that he can help us!" Lucy squealed. "You'll be able to see again!"

"If you are willing, Mr. Peachey, "we can schedule your first session for tomorrow."

"So soon?" Lucy asked.

"We need to move quickly," Dr. Robbins said.

Andy turned to Lucy.

"Can we have a minute?" Lucy asked, looking at the doctor.

"Of course, I'll be right outside."

They spoke when the doctor left.

"What should I do?" Andy asked.

Lucy reached for his hands and held them tightly. "Your *urgroossvadder* and *groossvadder* were old when their eyesight finally failed, but you are a young man, Andy. We have our whole lives ahead of us. This treatment will mean that you can see our *kinner*, teach them to identify a Red-breasted Nuthatch, and skate with me on the lake. You'll be able to see the world again, Andy."

"That's not what he said. He said there's a chance that it could get worse."

Lucy gathered her thoughts. "I would like to look into your eyes every night before we fall asleep knowing that you can see me."

Andy nodded. What'd he have to lose? He'd already lost his eyesight. Now was his chance to find it again. He had the surgery.

The three weeks that followed Andy's surgery were the longest he'd ever known. There was nothing to show whether it had worked. Daily, he scanned his wife's face, for it was what he most wanted to see, to contemplate God's best work. Still, as losing one's eyesight is a slow fade, its restoration is a tempered sharpening. It was in the third week that Andy noticed the familiar looked themselves again but with a halo. He contemplated his wife's face.

"You look like an angel!"

"What? Why?" Lucy asked.

"I am healed! Well, sort of. You have a halo about you. Everything does. Everything else looks like it's glowing, but you, you have the face of a cherub!"

Lucy shrieked. "It worked?"

Andy grinned. What a sight it is to behold one's beloved in haloed elation. He nodded. "*Ya.* Everything looks sharper and brighter than it has in years."

Lucy was delighted. She scrunched her nose and giggled. "You can see me?"

"Oh, *ya!*"

Andy could see Lucy's happiness, not just hear it. For the first time, he could see her with a heavenly glow enjoying life, enjoying his company, enjoying him. His presence was what made her smile. There is no prettier sight in the world than a happy girl. He was a man again.

"The glow will pass after a few more weeks," Dr Robbins said at their check-up.

"Thank you, Dr. Robbins," Lucy said, "for giving Andy the chance to see again."

"It was my pleasure." They all shook hands and said their goodbyes. "Now, you three look after yourselves," the doctor added.

Lucy smiled, placing a hand on her burgeoning belly. She had her wish: her *mann* would see his children's faces. *Truly, this little one will be a treasure from* Gott, she thought.

On the way home, Andy enjoyed the world outside. He

could see leaves again, with birds perched in their branches. "The world had never looked so beautiful. *Gott* has blessed me to be able to see His creation again." Turning to his bride, he added, "And His greatest work."

Lucy smiled. He had made her shy. She lay her head on his shoulder and gently touched his arm. "Dr. Robbins said you should not strain your eyes for the next few days," Lucy reminded him.

Andy chuckled. "You're cute when you're shy!"

Lucy pressed her head against him even harder, vainly hiding her blush.

"Don't worry," Andy said. "I'm making the most of the extra time that *Gott* has given me to see the beauties of His realm. When the time comes for my sight to fade again, I shall cherish the memories of this time."

Once they made it back to their community, Andy was eager to visit his favorite spot, the place where he'd realized that he wanted to marry Lucy.

"Come with me, Lucy," said Andy, holding out his hand. They walked toward the lake, now blue and shimmering from the sun's rays, reflecting the intense azure of the sky. Andy sat on the log and pulled Lucy down next to him. She sat contently, leaning against his arm. They listened quietly. They could hear the gentle cheep of the Downy Woodpecker, and up above them whistled the Cedar Waxwing. Then the air was full of the songs of warblers, woodcocks, and sparrows. The birds of spring had returned, as had Andy's hope.

"*Danki*, my *fraa*," Andy said tenderly.

Lucy's head popped up. "For what?"

"For giving me my sight again. Because of you, I can retake

my place at my *daed's* side working the land. Because you'll make me a *daed*. Because you have made me whole."

Thank you, readers!

Thank you for reading this book. It is important to me to share my stories with you and that you enjoy them. May I ask of you a favor? If you enjoyed this book, will you please take a moment to leave a review on Amazon and/or Goodreads? Thank you for your support!

Also, each week, I send my readers updates about my life as well as information about my new releases, freebies, promos, and book recommendations. If you're interested in receiving my weekly newsletter, please go to newsletter.sylviaprice.com, and it will ask you for your email. As a thank-you, you will receive a FREE exclusive short story that isn't available for purchase!

Blessings,
Sylvia

Books By This Author

The Christmas Arrival: An Amish Holiday Romance

Rachel Lapp is a young Amish woman who is the daughter of the community's bishop. She is in the midst of planning the annual Christmas Nativity play when newcomer Noah Miller arrives in town to spend Christmas with his cousins. Encouraged by her father to welcome the new arrival, Rachel asks Noah to be a part of the Nativity.

Despite Rachel's engagement to Samuel King, a local farmer, she finds herself irrevocably drawn to Noah and his carefree spirit. Reserved and slightly shy, Noah is hesitant to get involved in the play, but an unlikely friendship begins to develop between Rachel and Noah, bringing with it unexpected problems, including a seemingly harmless prank with life-threatening consequences that require a Christmas miracle.

Will Rachel honor her commitment to Samuel, or will Noah win her affections?

Join these characters on what is sure to be a heartwarming holiday adventure! Instead of waiting for each part to be released, enjoy the entire Christmas Arrival series in this exclusive collection!

Amish Love Through The Seasons (The Complete Series)

Featuring many of the beloved characters from Sylvia Price's bestseller, The Christmas Arrival, as well as a new cast of characters, Amish Love Through the Seasons centers around a group of teenagers as they find friendship, love, and hope in the midst of trials. This special boxed set includes the entire series, plus a bonus companion story, "Hope for Hannah's Love."

Tragedy strikes a small Amish community outside of Erie, Pennsylvania when Isaiah Fisher, a widower and father of three, is involved in a serious accident. When his family is left scrambling to pick up the pieces, the community unites to help the single father, but the hospital bills keep piling up. How will the family manage?

Mary Lapp, a youth in the community, decides to take up Isaiah's cause. She enlists the help of other teenagers to plant a garden and sell the produce. While tending to the garden, new relationships develop, but old ones are torn apart. With tensions mounting, will the youth get past their disagreements in order to reconcile and produce fruit? Will they each find love? Join them on their adventure through the seasons!

Included in this set are all the popular titles:
Seeds of Spring Love
Sprouts of Summer Love
Fruits of Fall Love
Waiting for Winter Love
"Hope for Hannah's Love" (a bonus companion short story)

Elijah: An Amish Story Of Crime And Romance

He's Amish. She's not. Each is looking for a change. What happens when God brings them together?

Elijah Troyer is eighteen years old when he decides to go on a delayed Rumspringa, an Amish tradition when adolescents venture out into the world to decide whether they want to continue their life in the Amish culture or leave for the ways of the world. He has only been in the city for a month when his life suddenly takes a strange twist.

Eve Campbell is a young woman in trouble with crime lords, and they will do anything to stop her from talking. After a chance encounter, Elijah is drawn into Eve's world at the same time she is drawn into his heart. He is determined to help Eve escape from the grips of her past, but his Amish upbringing has not prepared him for the dangers he encounters as he tries to pull Eve from her chaotic world and into his peaceful one.

Will Elijah choose to return to the safety of his family, or will the ways of the world sink their hooks into him? Do Elijah and Eve have a chance at a future together? Find out in this action-packed standalone novel.

Jonah's Redemption (Book 1)

Available for FREE on Amazon

Jonah has lost his community, and he's struggling to get by in the English world. He yearns for his Amish roots, but his past mistakes keep him from returning home.

Mary Lou is recovering from a medical scare. Her journey has impressed upon her how precious life is, so she decides to go on rumspringa to see the world.

While in the city, Mary Lou meets Jonah. Unable to understand his foul attitude, especially towards her, she makes every effort to share her faith with him. As she helps him heal from his past, an attraction develops.

Will Jonah's heart soften towards Mary Lou? What will God do with these two broken people?

Jonah's Redemption Boxed Set (Books 2-5, Epilogue, And Companion Story)

If you loved Jonah's Redemption: Book 1 (available for free on Amazon), grab the rest of the series in this special boxed set featuring Books 2-5, plus a bonus epilogue and companion story, "Jonah's Reminiscence."

Mary Lou's fiancé leaves her as soon as tragedy strikes. Unwilling to resent him, she chooses, instead, to find him. Her misfortunes pile up in her quest to return Jonah to the Amish faith, but she is undeterred, for God has given her a mission.

Will Mary Lou's faith be enough to help them get through the countless obstacles that are thrown their way? Do Jonah and Mary Lou have a chance at happiness?

Join Jonah and Mary Lou as they wrestle with love, a life worth living, and their unique faith in Christ. Enjoy the conclusion of Jonah's Redemption in this exclusive boxed set, with a bonus epilogue and companion story!

Songbird Cottage Beginnings (Pleasant Bay Prequel)

Available for FREE on Amazon

Set on Canada's picturesque Cape Breton Island, this book is perfect for those who enjoy new beginnings and countryside landscapes.

Sam MacAuley and his wife Annalize are total opposites. When Sam wants to leave city life in Halifax to get a plot of land on Cape Breton Island, where he grew up, his wife wants nothing to do with his plans and opts to move herself and their three boys back to her home country of South Africa.

As Sam settles into a new life on his own, his friend Lachlan encourages him to get back into the dating scene. Although he meets plenty of women, he longs to find the one with whom he wants to share the rest of his life. Will Sam ever meet "the one"?

Get to know Sam and discover the origins of the Songbird Cottage.

This is the prequel to the rest of the Pleasant Bay series.

The Songbird Cottage Boxed Set (Pleasant Bay Complete Series Collection)

Amazon bestselling author Sylvia Price's Pleasant Bay series is a feel-good read about family loyalties and second chances set on Canada's picturesque Cape Breton Island. This series is perfect for those who enjoy sweet romances and countryside landscapes. Enjoy all these sweet romance books in one collection for the first time!

Emma Copeland and her daughters, Claire and Isabelle, spend their summers at Songbird Cottage in Pleasant Bay, Nova Scotia. While there, Emma enjoys the company of her ruggedly handsome neighbor, Sam MacAuley, but when something happens between them, she vows never to return to Songbird Cottage.

When Emma turns fifty, she rushes into a marriage with smooth-talking Andrew Schönfeld, but when he suddenly dies, Emma loses everything.

With her life in shambles, and with nowhere else to stay, Emma returns to Songbird Cottage. Despite leaving without an explanation eighteen years ago, Sam is quick to Emma's aid when she arrives on Cape Breton.

As the beauty and peacefulness of Pleasant Bay begin to heal Emma, she gets some shocking news, and she discovers that she's unwelcomed at Songbird Cottage. Will she be able to piece her life back together and get another chance at happiness?

Join Emma Copeland and her daughters, Claire and Isabelle, get to know their family and neighbors, and explore the magic of Songbird Cottage.

Included in this set are all the popular titles:
The Songbird Cottage
Return to Songbird Cottage
Escape to Songbird Cottage
Secrets of Songbird Cottage
Seasons at Songbird Cottage

The Crystal Crescent Inn Boxed Set (Sambro Lighthouse Complete Series Collection)

Amazon bestselling author Sylvia Price's Sambro Lighthouse Series, set on Canada's picturesque Crystal Crescent Beach, is a feel-good read perfect for fans of second chances with a bit of history and mystery all rolled into one. Enjoy all five sweet romance books in one collection for the first time!

Liz Beckett is grief-stricken when her beloved husband of thirty-five years dies after a long battle with cancer. Her daughter and best friend insist she needs a project to keep her occupied. Liz decides to share the beauty of Crystal Crescent Beach with those who visit the beautiful east coast of Nova Scotia and prepares to embark on the adventure of her life. She moves into the converted art studio at the bottom of her garden and turns the old family home into The Crystal Crescent Inn.

One of her first visitors is famous archeologist, Merc MacGill, and he's not there to admire the view. The handsome bachelor believes there's an undiscovered eighteenth-century farmstead hidden inside the creeks and coves of Crystal Crescent, and Liz wants to help him find it.

But it's not all smooth sailing at the inn that overlooks the historic Sambro Lighthouse. No one has realized it yet, but the lives of everyone in Liz's family are intertwined with those first settlers who landed in Nova Scotia over two hundred and fifty years ago. Will they be able to unravel the mystery? Will the lives of Liz's two children be changed forever if they discover the link between the lighthouse and their old home?

Take a trip to Crystal Crescent Beach and join Liz, her family, and guests as they navigate the storms and calm waters of life and love under the watchful eye of the lighthouse and its secret.

About the Author

Now an Amazon bestselling author, Sylvia Price is an author of Amish and contemporary romance and women's fiction. She especially loves writing uplifting stories about second chances!

Sylvia was inspired to write about the Amish as a result of the enduring legacy of Mennonite missionaries in her life. While living with them for three weeks, they got her a library card and encouraged her to start reading to cope with the loss of television and radio, giving Sylvia a newfound appreciation for books.

Although raised in the cosmopolitan city of Montréal, Sylvia spent her adolescent and young adult years in Nova Scotia, and the beautiful countryside landscapes and ocean views serve as the backdrop to her contemporary novels.

After meeting and falling in love with an American while living abroad, Sylvia now resides in the US. She spends her days writing, hoping to inspire the next generation to read more stories. When she's not writing, Sylvia stays busy making sure her three young children are alive and well-fed.

Subscribe to Sylvia's newsletter at newsletter.sylviaprice.com to stay in the loop about new releases, freebies, promos, and more. As a thank-you, you will receive a FREE exclusive short story that isn't available for purchase!

Learn more about Sylvia at amazon.com/author/sylviaprice and goodreads.com/sylviapriceauthor.

Follow Sylvia on Facebook at facebook.com/sylviapriceauthor for updates.

Join Sylvia's Advanced Reader Copies (ARC) team at arcteam.sylviaprice.com to get her books for free before they are released in exchange for honest reviews.

Made in the USA
Middletown, DE
28 November 2021

53579907R00132